Dear Reader,

Smugglers, love, daring rescues.

It sounds like a swashbuckler, doesn't it? Actually that's the kind of story I wanted to create when I wrote *Blue Velvet*. It's a modern-day swashbuckler with dashing characters that I hope you like and want to accompany until they sail off into the sunset. This book is pure take-me-away escapism. I had just written *White Satin*, which concerned Olympic ice skating, and I suppose I was leaning toward getting away from the ice and cold.

So I have taken Beau Lantry to the tropics where he encounters Kate Gilbert, who is a bit of a swashbuckler herself and a woman like no other. The tropics become even sultrier when they fall in love. When danger explodes with hurricane-like force it only makes their passion stronger as they're drawn into the vortex.

And so the adventure begins. . . .

Iris Johansen

Books by Iris Johansen

IRIS JOHANSEN

Blue Velvet

BANTAM BOOKS
NEW YORK

2011 Bantam Books Mass Market Edition

Published in the United States by Bantam Books, an imprint of The Random House Publishing Group, a division of Random House, Inc., New York.

BANTAM BOOKS and the rooster colophon are registered trademarks of Random House, Inc.

Originally published in paperback in the United States by Bantam Books, an imprint of The Random House Publishing Group, a division of Random House, Inc., in 1985.

ISBN 978-0-345-52810-0
eBook ISBN 978-0-345-52811-7

Cover design: Eileen Carey

Printed in the United States of America

www.bantamdell.com

2   4   6   8   9   7   5   3   1

Bantam mass market edition: August 2011

For Dad,

For all the songs he sang me
For all the love he gave me.

Blue Velvet

ONE

"WHAT OTHER CHOICE do we have?" Kate argued, running her hand distractedly through her riot of short curls. Her eyes were fixed gloomily on the entrance to the waterfront tavern across the street. "We're caught between Scylla and Charybdis."

"Scylla and Charybdis?" Julio asked blankly.

"You know, the she monster of the sea and the whirlpool," Kate said, her gaze still on the door to Alvarez's Bar.

He didn't know, but then Kate was always referring to things he knew nothing about. "What Jeffrey calls between a rock and a hard place?"

Kate nodded. "If we don't go into that tavern and get Jeffrey, he's going to end up in the cockpit of the plane with a knife at his throat. Or they'll get him so drunk he'll tell them the location of the Cessna."

"If he doesn't pass out first," Julio suggested hopefully. "According to the bartender, he was pretty close to that point a few minutes ago."

"Then they'll wake him up and start all over," Kate said. She shook her head. "No, we've got to go in after him. Once we have him out of Ralph Despard's clutches we'll worry about getting him off Castellano."

"And how do we do that?" Julio asked, his lips curving in a skeptical smile. "Despard is alone at the table with Jeffrey now, but Simmons and a few of the other men are in one of the back rooms. If we make any move, they'll pour out of there and be all over us."

Kate bit her lower lip. "We can't make any obvious moves. I don't want them to realize that you're a part of Jeffrey's crew. You've always been away guarding the plane when Despard has visited Jeffrey at the cottage. As long as he doesn't know you exist, you'll be safe. I'll go in by myself."

"No, I will not permit it," Julio said firmly. He should have known how she'd react. Kate was as protective as a lioness with her cub about anyone she cared about and she cared about Jeffrey Brenden. Perhaps too much for her own good. In the four years he'd been with the two of them, he'd watched her nurse Brenden through hangovers, tease him into cheerfulness when he was depressed, and pull him out of scrapes. It never occurred to her to ask anything in return. Kate always gave with both hands. He couldn't criticize Jeffrey for taking from her; he himself had accepted her loving generosity and devoted affection on many occasions. However, he couldn't swallow the idea of her walking into that bar alone. "If it must be done, we'll do it together."

"No, I think I've come up with a way." Her brow was wrinkled in thought. "Did you check the location of the power box as I asked?"

He nodded. "It's outside and in the back."

"Good." She checked her wristwatch; it was just past midnight. "In ten minutes I want you to be at the power box. Give an on and off flicker as a warning for me. Everyone will think it's just a power surge. Then a minute later turn off the lights altogether and remove the fuse. Okay?"

"And what will you be doing while I'm playing with the fuse box?"

"I'll be at the table distracting Despard and trying to find a way to ease him out of the picture."

"Distracting?" Julio frowned. "I hope you don't mean what I think you mean. You wouldn't know how to handle a man like Despard."

"Oh, Julio, I said distract, not seduce! It shouldn't be all that difficult to divert the man for ten minutes. He's made a pass at me almost every time he's been at the cottage." She made a face. "Not that I'm anything special. He probably makes a pass at every woman under eighty."

But she *was* something special, Julio thought. Warm and loving with a clear bell-like honesty that he'd never known in any other woman. The idea of Despard so much as laying a hand on her made him a little sick. "I don't like it. You shouldn't even be in a bar like that."

"I've been in that bar plenty of times, as you know very well. And I can take care of myself," she added. "Heaven knows, I've had plenty of practice." That was certainly true, she thought ironically. Jeffrey was a dreamer, always chasing fantasies, and she trailed along behind trying to hold his feet on the ground and keep him from being too badly hurt. "And this is no exception. I'll be fine, Julio."

"I think I should . . ."

"No, Julio," she said with gentle firmness. "We'll do it the way I said. As soon as the lights go out, you dash around to the front door and come inside. I'll need help getting Jeffrey out of there. Until then, I want you to be as invisible as possible." She grinned impishly as her gaze traveled over his massive shoulders and intimidating bulk. "That should be enough of a challenge for you."

"Kate, it's too—"

"It's the only plan we've got," she interrupted. She looked at her watch again. "Ten minutes, remember." She started across the street without giving him a backward glance. Julio would keep her out here all night arguing and it would only end the same way. As she'd told him before, they were caught between Scylla and Charybdis.

The interior of the crowded bar was dim; the odors of whiskey and sweat mingled with the acrid-sweet aroma of marijuana. She paused a moment beside the long polished oak bar that was Hector Alvarez's pride and joy, her eyes searching anxiously around the room for the familiar gray-streaked head.

A woman at the corner table was lushly attractive and vaguely familiar, Kate noticed. Perhaps she'd even met her. Jeffrey liked company while he drank and the more attractive the company the better.

But the man the woman was with tonight certainly wasn't Jeffrey, though he looked as if he might be an American. He was dressed in black jeans and a short-sleeved knit shirt that was either navy or black. It was hard to tell in the dim light. But his hair was definitely a shining bronze. She was about to turn her attention to the other end of the room when the man glanced up swiftly as if suddenly aware that she was staring at him.

Dangerous. The thought came out of nowhere. There was a reckless curve to his well-shaped mouth and his smile had a mocking deviltry that was obviously very appealing to the bar girl next to him. His eyes narrowed on her and a thrill of uneasiness surged through her.

She glanced away. How stupid she was being. For a moment she'd actually felt more threatened by that stranger than she'd ever been by Ralph Despard. It must be because her nerves were stretched taut that her imagination was running away with her. She finally spotted Despard in the far corner. No wonder she hadn't seen Jeffrey, she thought gloomily. He was slumped forward, his curly head resting on the table. That was all she and Julio needed to make the situation perfect—a totally unconscious Jeffrey.

Well, they'd just have to cope.

"Hector lets me use a room in the back of the bar." The brunette's voice was soft and throatily inviting. Her hand beneath the table moved up on his thigh to caress him with a boldness that caused an immediate response and brought a glint of satisfaction to the Latin woman's eyes. "You see, I can please you very well. I know . . ."

Beau Lantry lost the thread of the exact extent of the knowledge the woman was confiding to him. What was her name? Liane, that was it. It wasn't her conversation that was important anyway. It was that lushly curved anatomy . . . and what that excitingly wicked hand was doing to his own anatomy beneath the table.

He'd dropped Barbara off at Barbados almost three weeks ago and he'd been without a woman ever since. He'd decided the instant he'd wandered into this waterfront tavern and the bar girl had smiled at him so invitingly that abstinence was going to end. She was clean and attractive and willing for anything, according to that husky murmur in his ear. It was exactly what he was looking for tonight. To have his frustration eased with no involvement and only a generous wad of bills left on the dresser in the morning.

He couldn't expect anything better without going farther afield into the town and he had no inclination to do that. He'd heard that the island republic of Castellano was a hangout for half the criminals in the Caribbean, and its government was almost as corrupt as its inhabitants. He wasn't about to wander around its principal city of Mariba and end up rolled and stabbed in an alley. No, he was very content right where he was. He'd stay in Hector's back room with Liane and in the morning go back to the *Searcher*. Then he'd tell Daniel to cast off and they'd be halfway to Trinidad by noon. That should relieve his captain. Daniel had been uncharacteristically cautious ever since their arrival in Mariba this afternoon. He'd refused to give the men shore leave and had stayed on board the ship himself.

As usual, he'd made no attempt to dissuade Beau from going ashore. Their compatibility was based on a policy of strict noninterference. Daniel never indicated by word or expression that he approved or disapproved of Beau's escapades . . . except when he indulged in a rare burst of roguish behavior himself and then he obviously approved very much indeed.

The woman was still murmuring in his ear and Beau supposed he should have been listening. She might have been talking money and he didn't want her to get huffy and think he wouldn't be generous with her. Still, he had all night and wasn't in any particular hurry. If he acted a bit reluctant perhaps it would spur her to greater inventiveness. His gaze drifted casually around the smoky barroom that was boringly similar to a hundred others he'd frequented in the last two years.

Blue eyes, clear and deep and utterly fearless.

He experienced a queer breathless shock as he met them across the room. He didn't think he'd ever seen anyone with eyes that reflected quite that degree of bold honesty before. He felt slightly annoyed at his overreaction. It must have been the unexpectedness of that blue gaze in a room full of dark-eyed Latins that had shaken him. After all, the woman possessing those eyes wasn't attractive enough to have disturbed him so. She appeared to be in her early twenties and her features were virtually nondescript except for those incredible eyes framed with long dark lashes. Her lips had a rather nice curve and a touch of vulnerability that was appealing, but her nose was definitely too turned up for beauty, much less glamour.

"You think she's pretty?" Liane asked sharply, following his gaze. "She's much too thin. Take those clothes off her and she would be all skin and bones."

"You think so?" Beau drawled, his gaze traveling over the woman standing by the bar. She was a little over average height and dressed in jeans faded by many washings to a pale white-blue. The loose man's shirt she wore was a blue of a slightly darker shade, its tails veiling the curve of her hips. She was no longer looking at him but at a table in the opposite corner of the room and there was a curious tenseness about her stance. "You can't really tell in that loose shirt and jeans. Do you know who she is?"

Liane shrugged. "Kate something or other. I have seen her in here a few times." She leaned forward, revealing a bounty of lush cleavage. "She is not nearly as popular as me and she would have to take you somewhere else. I am the only one Hector will let use his back room."

"I'm sure you've earned his generosity," he said, removing her hand from his thigh. Suddenly her curves seemed a trifle overblown and her attractiveness a little too common for his taste.

The woman called Kate was walking toward

the corner table now and she moved with a free graceful stride that was very pleasing. Her short curly hair, sun-tipped here and there to pale gold, was an acorn brown and as baby soft and silky clean as in a shampoo commercial. Her skin appeared that soft, too, he mused, lifting a glass of ginger ale to his lips. He suddenly felt an urgent desire to touch that skin.

"You will go with me, then?" Liane asked with a sultry smile.

"What?" he asked. He set his glass down and rose to his feet. "Perhaps another time." He placed a large bill on the table and strolled in the same direction as the blue-eyed, winsome Kate.

That silky-soft skin was too appealing to pass up and he could visualize how delicious she would be with those boyish clothes removed. Thin, perhaps, as Liane claimed, but there was a pert femininity to that little derriere that was very tempting. And he'd never been one to resist temptation when it beckoned so seductively.

The only problem was the lady seemed to have a target in mind. The table she halted at was occupied by two dark-haired men. There was a half-empty bourbon bottle before them; one of the men had passed out. At least he wouldn't be any competition for Kate's favors, Beau thought. It was the one with the little pig eyes who was looking up at her with a grin on his dark bearded face that he'd have to remove from the scene. Money? If not, he might have a more interesting evening than he'd planned. There was suddenly a touch of recklessness in Beau's smile as he quickened his steps. He had a hunch that a night with silky-skinned Kate might be worth a little minor mayhem.

She was saying something to the bearded man now and the man's hand was reaching out and casually fondling her buttocks. She appeared to be paying no attention to the intimacy but Beau found he was experiencing a curiously possessive resentment. He shrugged it off impatiently. For heaven's sake, all he had in mind was a one-night stand with an accommodating bar girl. What the hell was the matter with him?

However, there was still a lingering edge to that possessiveness as he stopped beside the table. The woman broke off in midsentence and those startling blue eyes widened in surprise as she glanced up at him.

He sketched a mocking little bow. "Sorry to disturb you in the middle of negotiations. I just didn't want you to get too far along before I could enter my own invitation, or should I say, bid."

"Buzz off," the bearded man snapped out. He straightened slowly in his chair. "The lady and I are just reaching an understanding."

"But that's because she hasn't heard my offer," Beau drawled, and looked at Kate, his gaze full of a smoldering promise. "I'm prepared to be more than generous. Come with me, Kate." His voice was coaxing. "You won't regret it."

She looked away, but not before he'd seen a glimmer of fear in her eyes that puzzled him. "Go away," she said jerkily. "Ralph is right, we're having a discussion."

The man called Ralph gave a low laugh of triumphant satisfaction, his hand once more moving in a caress on Kate's bottom. "You see, you're not wanted and I definitely am." He glanced up at her. "Aren't I, Kate?"

"That's right. How could you doubt it, Ralph? You've always told me how good we'd be for each other."

"We'd be better together," Beau said softly.

"And I'll give you whatever you want. Tell me what you want and it's yours."

"Please." She moistened her lips nervously, then smiled down at Ralph.

God, she had a lovely smile. It lit up her entire face with such warmth that it made one forget she wasn't really beautiful. Beau found himself resenting the smile she was giving the other man more than he had that hand of his on her bottom. The reaction was just as crazy and totally irrational as all his other responses. He knew he should forget about her and go back to Liane. He was obviously going to have to fight both her and her chosen mark for the evening to obtain her services for himself. He also couldn't say much for her taste in men. The fellow had a distinctly shifty look in those little pig eyes. The eyes reminded him vaguely of someone. George. That was it. Good old greedy gut, Uncle George. He felt his antagonism swell with a sudden intensity that had nothing to do with logic. The Uncle Georges of the world managed to snatch quite enough for themselves without having it handed to them on a plate. There was no way he was going to let pig eyes here get his hands on anything he wanted. And he was beginning to want Kate more every second.

As the tense silence lengthened, Kate glanced furtively at the leather-banded watch on her wrist and then stared at Beau. "Please go," she ordered. "Now!"

"Not until you go with me."

The bearded man's hand dropped away from Kate's hip and he scowled menacingly. "I told you to—"

The lights flickered and Kate's face went tense with strain and exasperation. "Oh, damn!" She reached for the bourbon bottle in the middle of the table. "Triple damn!" She brought the bottle down forcefully on Ralph's head. "I told you to leave," she wailed at Beau as Ralph's eyes glazed over and he slumped forward, knocked unconscious by Kate's blow. "Why couldn't you do it, blast it?"

The lights went out and sudden darkness threw the patrons into an uproar. Their shouts muted the screech of hurriedly pushed back chairs and were followed by angry curses as they stumbled around.

"I'll remember next time how strongly you

tend to reinforce your wishes," Beau said dryly. "You didn't have to get rid of him yourself, you know. I would have done it for you. Besides the fact that he was in our way, he reminded me very unpleasantly of Uncle George."

"Oh, be quiet," Kate muttered. "You almost ruined everything. I was trying to keep his guard down and you had him practically bristling."

Beau's eyes were becoming accustomed to the darkness now and he could see that Kate was moving around the table toward the gray-haired man who'd remained in blissful alcoholic unconsciousness during the entire episode. What the devil was she up to now?

"Kate?"

The voice was strong and masculine and came from the direction of the door.

"Over here," Kate called. She was tugging at the gray-haired man's chair. "Straight forward and all the way to the back."

"May I help?" Beau asked politely.

"Just stay out of the way," Kate said crossly. "You've been enough bother. We don't have much time left." A huge hulking shadow appeared at her side.

"Kate?" It was the voice from the doorway, a trifle subdued now.

"I'm standing right beside him, Julio." Kate's tone was relieved. "I've taken care of Despard but someone is bound to find a flashlight soon. We've got to get Jeffrey out of here before Simmons comes barreling out of that back room."

"Don't worry. I'll have him out of here and safe in just a minute." Julio's soothing answer had a trace of a Spanish accent as he bent forward and lifted the smaller man onto his shoulder in a fireman's carry. "You go ahead and make sure there's no one in front of me."

"I'll run interference," Beau offered. He was becoming more intrigued every moment. "Providing you're not plotting any dire fate for that inanimate object you're carrying. You're not planning on committing murder as well as assault, I hope?"

The enormous shadow that was Julio froze. "Who's that?"

"No one important," Kate answered impatiently. "He's no threat, Julio. Let's just get out of here."

"Yes, by all means," Beau agreed. "Before

what's-his-name comes barreling out of that back room." He turned and started for the front entrance. "Follow me, Julio."

He didn't turn to see if he was being obeyed but moved lithely through the cursing, milling throng, thrusting people out of the way with ruthless efficiency until he came to the door that Julio had left open. As he went through it, he glanced over his shoulder and saw the giant close on his heels with his unwieldy burden. The streetlight on the corner cast a shadowy illumination over the man and Beau pursed his lips in a soundless whistle. Julio had to be six feet five at least and built like a tackle for the Rams.

"There's an alley about a block down," Kate said. "We can stay there until the coast is clear." She was turning left and leading the way. "Oh, hurry, Julio!"

Beau answered. "We're right behind you."

"Not you." She cast him an exasperated glance over her shoulder. "Go away!"

"I can't do that," Beau said lightly. "How do I know what you're planning on doing to our friend here? You might be thinking of throwing him off the dock and then I'd be an accomplice to murder." He shook his head. "No, I really think I'd better tag along and protect my interests."

"We're not going to do any such thing," Kate said indignantly. "Can't you see we're rescuing him?"

"Was that what you were doing?" Beau's brow arched quizzically. "It was all a little muddled back there. The only obvious victim appeared to be our friend Ralph." There was a touch of tiger in his smile. "Not that I'm objecting to his disposal, you understand. I was planning on taking him out anyway."

"Well, I did it for you," Kate answered as she turned into a pitch-dark alley that stank of garbage and wet cardboard boxes. "But Despard may remember you when he wakes up so you'd be wise to leave Castellano before he does. He's not going to be at all pleased with any of us."

"How unfortunate," Beau murmured. "And I was hoping for such a pleasant relationship."

They'd reached the end of the alley and Kate motioned for Julio to put his burden down in an alcove formed by a deeply recessed side door.

"You're very amused by all this, aren't you? You may not find it so entertaining if Despard realizes that you helped us. He's a very dangerous man."

"I must admit your little play certainly livened up a boring evening," he said coolly. "Would you care to tell me why this Despard is such a threat?"

"He's a drug runner," Kate said. "One of the biggest in the Caribbean and he has contacts high up in the government of Castellano. Your American citizenship might protect you from the government, but not from Despard's men." She paused uncertainly. "You *are* American, aren't you? You have a very odd accent."

"I'm from Virginia." There was a thread of indignation in his voice. "And there's nothing odd about a Southern accent. It's Yankees who talk funny."

"Is that what it is?" she asked as she knelt beside the man Julio had propped against the alcove wall. She fumbled in the pocket of her jeans and suddenly there was the flickering flame of a lighter illuminating the darkness. "I've never heard one before."

Never heard a Southern accent before? Yet she herself sounded as American as apple pie. "Where are you from?"

"All around," she said vaguely, lifting the unconscious man's eyelid. "He's dead to the world, Julio. There's no way we can get him all the way through town and into the forest without you carrying him." She sat back on her heels. "And someone's bound to notice and report back to Despard. He owns almost everyone in town."

Julio dropped to his knees beside her. "So what do we do?"

She pressed a hand to her temple. "How do I know? Let me think a minute."

"Perhaps I could offer a suggestion or two," Beau said. "I take it your unconscious friend here is now on the run from both the local authorities and this Despard and you're looking for a place to hide him until you can get him off the island. Is that correct?" When she nodded, he continued. "I have a safe place not two blocks from here. I can also guarantee to get both him and the two of you off Castellano and as far away as Trinidad if you like." He arched an eyebrow inquiringly. "Interested?"

She nodded slowly. "Where is this place?"

"I own a schooner docked in the harbor. All you have to do is say the word and we'll take your fugitive there."

Her brilliant blue eyes were clear and direct in the flickering glow of the lighter. "And what word is that?" she asked quietly.

His lips curved in a mocking smile. "Yes," he said. "You only have to say yes to that proposition I put to you in the bar. Not a very high price to pay for your friend's safety, is it?"

She was very still for a moment. "No, not a very high price." She turned away so he could see only her profile as she gazed tenderly down at the face of the unconscious man. "Cheap, really."

"Proposition?" Julio asked with a suspicious frown.

"Don't worry, Julio," Kate said quietly. "The gentleman and I understand each other."

"But what kind of—"

"I said it was okay." Kate's tone brooked no argument. "Forget it. We have more important things to be concerned about right now." Her eyes met Beau's. "All right. It's a bargain."

"Good." He felt a thrill of excitement out of all proportion to the victory he'd won. Excitement, he wondered cynically, or was it merely pure lust? Perhaps a little of both. "Now that we have that out of the way perhaps introductions are in order." He inclined his head in a sketch of a bow. "Beau Lantry, at your service."

"Kate Gilbert. And this is Julio Rodriguez."

"And our inebriated friend?"

Kate gently brushed a lank strand of hair from the unconscious man's forehead. "Jeffrey Brenden."

"A relation?" He was feeling that same surge of unreasonable jealousy he'd known when she'd smiled at Despard in the bar.

She shook her head. "No relation, just a friend."

"Well, I suggest we get your 'friend' to his safe and cozy berth."

"It's too soon for Julio to move him yet. They might be spotted," she said. "But I think we can go now." She flicked him a cool glance. "I have a job to do before I leave Castellano. I want you to help me."

"The cache?" Julio asked, shaking his head.

"It's too dangerous, Kate. If you're caught even near that place Despard's men will kill you."

She ignored him, her gaze fixed with quiet challenge on Beau. "He's right. It's very dangerous. That should amuse you even more than what happened in the bar. Will you come with me?"

"Is it illegal or just immoral?" Beau asked lightly.

"Neither, except on Castellano. In fact, the U.S. Customs Service would probably give you a medal." She smiled slightly. "We're going to burn up about six million dollars' worth of cocaine."

Beau gave a low whistle. "Well, I suppose I've got to protect my investment. Besides, I've always been fond of medals. I haven't won one for years. I believe it's time I tried my luck again." He turned to Julio. "The schooner is called the *Searcher*. The captain is Daniel Seifert and all you have to do is tell him that Beau sent you. He'll take it from there."

Julio frowned uncertainly. "He won't ask any questions?"

Beau shook his head. "He may be a little curious, but he won't object. Daniel's used to my way of doing things by now."

That clear blue gaze was on his face again, this time gravely searching. "And this type of thing isn't all that unusual for you, is it? You like the excitement of skating on thin ice."

He suddenly chuckled. "Funny you should say that. I haven't given a thought to skating for two years." His lips quirked. "But I have to admit that thin ice definitely makes things more interesting." He stood up and reached out his hand to pull her to her feet. "Shall we go and see if we can find some?"

Two

THE GLOW FROM the streetlight at the end of the alley revealed that his eyes weren't really brown as she'd first thought. They were hazel with odd golden flecks about the pupil that gave him an air of reckless instability. They were gleaming now with excitement—and that recklessness— as he looked down at her. "Is it too much to ask where this cache of cocaine is located?"

"Only a few blocks away. Despard and his men are using a small deserted warehouse close to the waterfront for storage. They were going to transport the cocaine by sea but they weren't able to hijack the yacht they wanted." Kate glanced up and down the street cautiously before turning right and motioning to Beau to follow. "It shouldn't take us more than fifteen minutes to get there."

"Providing we don't run into trouble." He fell into step with her, easily accommodating his long strides to her short but rapid steps. "It appears we've given your criminal cohorts the slip, but that doesn't mean they won't catch up with us."

"You don't have to sound so hopeful," she said, shooting him an indignant glance. "You may be enjoying all this enormously, but I assure you I'm taking it very seriously." She frowned. "And Despard isn't any cohort of ours. I can't stand the man. He's a damn cockatrice."

"A what?" he asked blankly.

"A cockatrice," she repeated impatiently. "You know, the mythical serpent that could kill with a look."

"Oh, of course." Beau's lips were twitching. "How could I have forgotten? Please forgive me. I can see how lumping you together with this cockatrice would be a terrible faux pas. It just seemed reasonable to assume you'd been partners with Despard and had a falling out."

"No, Jeffrey never takes partners. He works alone." She gave him a fierce glance. "And he's not really a criminal. Not like those cockatrices."

"Really? Well, what kind of criminal is he?" Beau asked idly. "I gather he was scheduled to transport this cocaine illegally into the U.S. I believe that constitutes smuggling and the last I heard that was considered very criminal indeed. Are you saying he's not a smuggler?"

"No." She frowned unhappily. "Yes. Oh, I guess he is, but he doesn't look at it that way. He never smuggles drugs or liquor or anything that could actually hurt someone."

"It's unfortunate that the authorities don't regard the smuggling of things that don't actually hurt someone as all right."

"Jeffrey is a throwback to another era. He sees himself as some sort of Henry Morgan or Jean Laffite." She shrugged helplessly. "He regards smuggling as a sort of modern-day gentleman's adventurous pastime."

"And do you feel the same way?"

She shook her head. "No," she said simply. "But I know he believes it, and that's enough for me."

"Such devotion." There was a barbed sting to his mockery. "Your lover must be very grateful for such an understanding mistress, as well as such an enterprising one. How often do you drag him out of situations like that one tonight?"

Her eyes widened in surprise. "Jeffrey isn't my lover." It never occurred to her he would think that but it was also obvious that for some reason the idea didn't sit well with him.

His gaze flew swiftly to her face. "Then the other one?"

"Julio?" She had to laugh. "Julio's only eighteen."

"He looks older. I would have said he was at least twenty-five." His lips quirked again. "And an old lady like you isn't interested in younger men, I take it?"

"Julio's been through a lot. His life has been very difficult." Her expression was suddenly sober. "We're all friends, that's all. We take care of each other." Her clear blue eyes held a childlike gravity as they looked up at him. "Haven't you ever had a woman as a friend?"

"Once." He grimaced. "A very special lady, but unfortunately six years' bondage went along with that friendship, so I've shied away from even the thought of seeing a woman in that light ever since." His smile was frankly sensual. "I prefer that the bondage be short term and gratifying to both parties. Like the very satisfying terms we recently negotiated."

She nodded, her expression thoughtful. "Yes, I can see you'd hate any curb on your freedom." She sensed there was something wild—a charged restlessness that was almost explosive, perhaps— beneath his droll speech and behavior. "I think perhaps you may be the type of man Jeffrey has tried to be all his life. You don't have any pirate blood in your ancestry by any chance?"

"Well, now that you mention it, there was a Lantry who was a privateer during the War of 1812," he said lightly. "A very efficient one I understand. He founded the family fortune on booty he wrested from the British." He winked. "As well as the French, the Spanish, the Dutch, and everyone else on the high seas. All in the name of patriotism, you know."

"You and Jeffrey would probably get along very well. You're obviously kindred spirits."

She suddenly smiled at him and he inhaled sharply. Lord, that was a lovely smile, he realized once again. It was like a ray of warm sunlight on a cold winter's day.

"It's more than likely he'll try to talk you into going into business with him," she continued. "Would you be interested?"

"Smuggling?" He shook his head. "There's only one aspect of your Jeffrey's little operation that intrigues me—and I'm looking at her." His gaze was lingering on the high curve of her breasts outlined beneath the blue chambray work shirt. "Though not nearly enough of her at the present time."

Kate felt a heat start in her breasts and begin to spread slowly through her body. It was as if he'd unbuttoned her shirt and caressed her. Her response to his look was so raw, so primitive that it shocked her. If a glance from those odd golden eyes could do that to her, then what would it be like when he actually touched her?

Blue Velvet

She was suddenly glad that the street was lit only by the occasional dim street lamp. There was no way she wanted him to see the warm flush that was mantling her cheeks or to notice that her breathing had become a little shallow. She glanced away hurriedly. "When?"

His brow lifted inquiringly. "When?"

"When do you want me to go to bed with you?" she asked clearly. "And how many times before you feel the bargain is fulfilled? I'd like to know, please."

"You don't believe in being coyly retiring, do you?" There was a trace of annoyance mixed with the amusement in his voice. "Would you like me to draw up a contract and set out precise terms and conditions?" He suddenly chuckled. "That could be pretty erotic! We could list all the positions I'd require and then go on to—"

"I just like to have things open and above-board," she interrupted. She could feel her cheeks burn even hotter. "I don't think that's so amusing."

There was an endearing little-girl awkwardness about her that aroused a queer protective tenderness in him. "No, it's not really amusing," he said gently. "I've been accused of having a rather puckish sense of humor upon occasion. You'll get used to it. As for your passion for laying the cards on the table, let's see if I can satisfy you." His eyes twinkled roguishly. "I really didn't mean that as a double entendre. Now that it's popped out, though, let me promise I *will* satisfy you as well. Let's see, your first question was 'when.'" His smile faded and she was once more aware of the smoldering sensuality below the surface. "As soon as possible. I'd take you right now if I could. I want you so much I'm aching with the need of you." He glanced down into her startled eyes. "It's surprising the hell out me too," he said grimly. "I can't remember ever feeling quite this degree of sexual urgency. Particularly when the woman in question is selling her body for a price tag that could possibly get me killed." Then the grimness was gone, replaced by that now familiar mockery. "As for the rest, don't worry about it. I'm not particularly kinky and I won't do anything you won't enjoy." He reached out and touched his index finger to her cheek. "And I'm sorry, but I'm not going to set a limit on the times I'm going to make love to you. I have a hunch it may go on for a long, long time. It may even develop into a full-scale affair. I'll require you to stay with me as long as I want you. Period. Is your friend Jeffrey's safety worth that degree of commitment or does that change the picture?"

Her cheek felt as if it were burning beneath that light touch and her heart was accelerating crazily. She tried to hold her voice steady. "He's worth it." She edged away so that his disconcerting hand no longer touched her face. "And no, it doesn't change anything. I just wanted to know."

"Well, now you do." She could sense the tension ebbing out of him as he relaxed. "And we can get on to accomplishing this little task you've set up to test my mettle." He made a face. "I can't say it wasn't a clever move. If I get killed by these charming gentlemen you're associated with, you won't have to pay off."

"Don't say that," she said sharply, her eyes wide with fright. "Nothing's going to happen to you. I'd never have insisted you come if I'd thought there was really a chance you might be harmed. I only brought you along because I need a lookout. I'll do everything myself." She drew a deep shaky breath. "You needn't be afraid. I'll take care of you."

She meant it. He'd started to chuckle but the laughter vanished as he met that childlike earnestness in her eyes. He supposed he should have been a little insulted that she'd presumed he needed her protection. Somehow, though, he wasn't. He was touched and moved and suddenly feeling that inexplicable tenderness once again. "Thank you," he said with grave courtesy. "I'm sure you could protect me very well, but I never did like a bystander's role. Perhaps I can find something to do to make things a bit more interesting." As she opened her lips to protest, he asked quickly, "How close are we to the warehouse?"

"We're almost there. It's just around the corner and down a few buildings. It's set off by itself, thank heavens. We don't have to worry about anything else catching on fire."

"I'm sure the citizens of Mariba will be grateful for that," Beau drawled. "They may even put up a statue in the city square in your honor." His tongue moistened his lower lip in mock lasciviousness. "In fact, if you'll promise to pose in the nude, I'd probably commission it myself."

"Oh, be quiet." She couldn't keep a little smile from tugging at her lips. The man was completely impossible. "This isn't funny, Beau. I wouldn't be here if it were."

"No, you're angry at Despard for trying to victimize your friend, Brenden, and you want to get some of your own back. A rather dangerous form of revenge, don't you think?"

"Revenge?" She shook her head. "I'd be pretty stupid to run this kind of risk for revenge."

"Then, why?"

"The drugs," she said simply. "I hate them. I've seen what they can do." Her eyes were haunted. "Drugs are cheaper here and in South America, you know. Dealers aren't able to get the high prices they can in the States. That's why they export them." She shivered. "And if they can't export them, they sell them to whoever will buy. Have you ever seen a nine-year-old junkie? I have, and I never want to again. If I could burn every cache of heroin and cocaine in the whole damn world, I'd do it."

That streak of maternal protectiveness again,

Beau thought. First Brenden, then himself, and now the whole damn world! That tenderness he'd known before returned with poignant intensity. What the hell was she doing to him? He forcibly pulled his gaze from those disconcertingly honest eyes and turned away. "Well, we can make a start tonight anyway. Let's get the show on the road. Do you know what the setup is or do we have to reconnoiter?"

"There are only two guards and they're both inside." She frowned. "Unless they've changed their arrangements since last week. I followed Despard here from the cottage and then took a look around back. There's a large window in the rear, but it's locked. I checked that out."

"A back door?"

"Yes, but they keep it locked too."

His glance traveled once more over her fitted jeans and loose chambray shirt. "I don't suppose you're carrying a forty-five or a hand grenade taped to your waist?" he asked politely. "Just how did you intend to accomplish this coup?"

She shuffled uncomfortably. "I would have thought of something," she said defensively. "I'm very resourceful."

"I've noticed that," he said dryly. "It appears you're very impulsive as well. Next time, let me do the groundwork, okay? Tactical maneuvers have a tendency to work a hell of a lot better if you have a plan."

Next time? "Well, I did make one preparation," she said triumphantly. "Two days ago I stashed a can of gasoline in a cardboard box in the trash heap at the back and covered it up with newspapers."

"Well, that's something. Providing the local sanitation company hasn't collected their trash."

She shook her head positively. "Not on Castellano. There's no sanitation department in Mariba. Everyone takes care of removing his own garbage."

"No wonder that alley was so unpleasantly aromatic." His eyes narrowed thoughtfully. "Do those guards know who you are?"

"They've seen me around Mariba, I suppose," she said. "It's a fairly small city and Despard's been trying to talk Jeffrey into running the coke for over a week."

"Then we may have a chance, after all," he said. "Can I get around back this way?" He indicated a small passageway a few yards ahead and at her nod, said, "Give me that lighter you were using in the alley."

He was being very demanding, she thought resentfully. She wasn't used to anyone else taking control and she wasn't at all sure she liked it. Still, there was such command in his demeanor she found herself digging into her pocket and putting the lighter into his hand. "What are you going to do with it?"

"I'll think of something. I'm very resourceful," he said, mimicking her mischievously. "Give me fifteen minutes and go pound on the front door. Then find a way of distracting the attention of the guards until I get in the back."

"But I told you there's no way to break—"

"Let me worry about that." He was striding swiftly toward the passage. "You just concentrate on distracting them," he hissed over his shoulder.

"That seems to be my role for the evening." She sighed. "First Despard, and now his merry henchmen."

He stopped and turned to stare at her. "I noticed how you were 'distracting' Despard." His voice was suddenly crackling with menace. "His hands were all over you. I won't put up with that now that you're mine. Sex is definitely out, Kate. Find some other method or you might discover I'm a hell of a lot more difficult to deal with than Despard."

Before she could answer he'd disappeared down the passage leaving her to gaze after him with indignation and a touch of fear. She had a fleeting memory of her first impression tonight in the bar. That mocking, cynical façade obviously masked an extremely complex man and she had an idea he might prove to be just as dangerous as she'd originally thought. Not that he could prove any threat to her, she assured herself staunchly. After she'd paid off her debt she'd probably never see the man again. They were strangers drawn together by a chance set of bizarre circumstances and, once Lantry had what he wanted, he probably wouldn't be able to rid himself of her fast enough. Possessiveness would no doubt vanish as quickly as his other emotions. As for his lovemaking . . . no, she wouldn't think about that. It brought a queer melting sensation to the pit of her stomach and

an aching tingle between her thighs that confused her terribly. She'd face that when she had
to. Right now she had something else to think
about.

She glanced down at her watch. Five more
minutes. What on earth did Beau have in mind?
Well, she'd find out soon enough. She only
hoped that whatever he tried would be startling
enough to catch them off guard.

His ploy was every bit as startling as she could
have wished, and more.

The two Latin guards were gazing at her in
half-suspicious puzzlement while she sobbed
with an authenticity of which she wouldn't have
dreamed she was capable. "But you must know
where Ralph is," she cried hysterically. "They
told me at Alvarez's he was coming here. He said
I could come to him if I needed him, that he'd
take care of me." Tears rolled down her cheeks.
"Jeffrey beat me . . ."

Suddenly there was an explosive crash of
splintering glass and breaking wood and she
didn't have to fake her dazed befuddlement as

she saw a large garbage can catapult through the window at the opposite end of the warehouse. The can was immediately followed by Beau, who dove headfirst through the window, carrying a blazing makeshift torch in each hand. Tucking his head under, he hit the rough wood floor in a rolling somersault that would have done justice to a circus acrobat. He was halfway across the room when he sprang lithely to his feet, the torches still aflame.

Both guards had whirled at the first sound but had been so dumbfounded they'd stood transfixed by Beau's unorthodox entrance. Now he was only a few yards away and they were jolted into action.

"Madre de Dios!" The short burly guard bounded forward and the taller one reached for the revolver tucked in the waist of his jeans.

Kate reacted without thinking, leaping for the man's gun arm and hanging on with all her strength while he tried to shake her off. She heard a low guttural cry and the thud of a body hitting the floor behind her. Oh, dear heaven, was it Beau?

"Puta!" snarled the man whose arm she was

clinging to like a limpet. His other fist shot out with vicious force and she felt a blinding pain in her temple. Her grasp automatically loosened and he shook her off easily, drawing the gun and backhanding her with the barrel. For a moment she was conscious of pressure but not pain and then there was an instant of darkness as the room whirled around her.

"You son of a bitch!" Beau's voice was so laden with icy menace that it shocked her into awareness again. So, it was the other man who'd fallen to the floor, she realized dazedly, for Beau was now right next to them. His eyes were blazing in golden fury and his face was granite hard. He was still carrying one of the torches in his hand and with one sweeping movement he enveloped the man's gun arm in flame!

The man's shriek of agony was terrible; he dropped the gun and started to beat frantically at the loose sleeve of his cotton shirt. His whimpering moans ended abruptly as the edge of Beau's hand swooped down in a karate chop to the neck, dropping the man in his tracks.

"Are you all right?" Beau asked, his voice rough with concern.

She was staring down at the unconscious man at their feet. The violence in Beau had erupted so quickly and brutally she was dazed. She noticed that the guard's shirt was still smoldering. She asked a little jerkily, "Hadn't we better put it out?"

"I ought to let the bastard burn up," Beau said savagely. "Did he hurt you?"

"No," she lied, moistening her lips. In that moment she believed Beau *would* have committed murder if she'd answered in the affirmative. "I'm just shaken up a little. I'll be fine in a minute." She laughed shakily. "But the sight of that smoldering shirt isn't helping very much. Please put it out."

He shrugged. "I don't know why you're so concerned." He reached down and carelessly beat out the last of the tiny licking sparks that remained. "This scum was probably first in line pushing the drugs on those kids you were so worried about."

"Maybe." Her gaze went to the short burly man lying unconscious across the room. "You're evidently very good at karate." She noticed the burning torch beside the squat body of the other guard. "Did you burn him too?"

"Not much. I tossed the torch at him as he was charging me. It hit him in the chest and bounced off." He smiled tigerishly. "But it threw him off balance long enough for me to get close. It's surprising how fire frightens people. I suppose it's because we've all had experience of the pain of being burned at some time or other."

"I suppose so." She straightened carefully. If she didn't move her head quickly, she found it didn't hurt so much. "It was very clever of you to think to use those torches as weapons." She smiled with an effort at lightness. "You were very impressive diving through that window like a circus acrobat."

"I was aiming more at Burt Lancaster in *The Crimson Pirate*," Beau drawled. To her relief the charged menace in him seemed to be dissipating.

"The Crimson Pirate?"

"A swashbuckling movie classic. Didn't you ever see it?"

She automatically shook her head and then wished she hadn't as the room suddenly darkened. "No, I've never seen a movie," she said vaguely. "Though I've read about them, of course. Jeffrey tells me I haven't missed much."

"Never seen . . ." He trailed off, his lips tightening grimly. "It would have been better if your precious Jeffrey had let you judge for yourself."

"You think so?" she asked absently. "Those plastine bags piled in that corner must be the coke. I'll punch holes in the bags while you drag the guards outside, then get the gasoline can."

"If you insist. Though I'd prefer to leave our friend here in the funeral pyre." He dropped the torch in his hand on the floor and drew a pristine handkerchief from his back pocket. "Turn around."

"What?"

"Turn around." He didn't wait for her to obey but stepped behind her and slipped the handkerchief over her nose and mouth and proceeded to tie it securely. "I don't suppose it occurred to you that fumes from the coke could possibly be intoxicating or even lethal?"

"Are they?"

"I don't have any idea but we're not taking any chances. I'll see if I can find something on one of the guards to use as my own mask." He knelt beside the squat unconscious guard and searched through the man's pockets. "Ah, this may be useful." His thumb pressed a switch on the pocketknife he'd taken from the man and a wicked-looking blade appeared. He handed it to her shaft first. "Get going. I'll have the gasoline in here on the double."

That touch of arrogance again! But she was in no condition to protest at the moment. She silently accepted the knife and turned away. Crossing the room with slow cautious steps, she heard the slithering sound of the guards' bodies being pulled across the wooden floor and out the front door. She knelt beside the plastine bags and began to punch a hole in each bag as quickly as possible. Her hands were shaking a little and there seemed to be hundreds of them. Long minutes passed as she punched bag after bag. Why the devil couldn't the coke have been packaged in bigger bags? These seemed to be kilo-sized . . . and it sure took a lot of kilos at 2.2 pounds to make up a $6 million cocaine deal.

"All set?" Beau was standing beside her, the gasoline can in his hand and a handkerchief tied over his nose and mouth.

She punctured the last two bags, dropped the pocketknife on the pile and very carefully got to her feet. "All set."

"Outside," Beau ordered, turning her around and giving her a push toward the door. "I'll be with you in a minute." Then he was pouring the gasoline over the piles of coke.

She took a few automatic steps toward the door before she stopped short. What was she doing? This was her job, not Beau Lantry's. She turned back and saw Beau throw the gasoline can down, scoop up the burning torch from the floor, step back and hurl it on the pile of coke. It burst into flame! Beau wheeled and dashed for the door, his arm encircling her as he passed, carrying her with him. "I told you to get out of here," he growled with barely restrained exasperation. "Why the hell didn't you?"

"The whole thing was my idea. I couldn't leave you alone to do my job."

"Couldn't you?" There was an odd searching flicker in his eyes as he paused a few yards outside the door to remove her mask and then his own. "No, I don't think you could, Kate."

He was gazing at her so intently she felt a tinge

of uneasiness. "Hadn't we better get away from here before the building goes up? It's bound to bring the rest of Despard's men on the run."

He looked away. "You're right." His hand was beneath her elbow guiding her away from the warehouse. "Let's go."

The warm humid air was striking her face like a smothering wet rag. She'd hoped it would help clear the mist that was interfering with her thought processes but it only seemed to increase the heavy lethargy she was experiencing. "What did you say the name of your ship is?"

"The *Searcher*." His eyes were once more narrowed keenly on her face. "It shouldn't take long to get to the docks from here, should it?"

"No, not very long," she said vaguely. "*Searcher* is an odd name for a ship. Most of them are named after women. No one seems to know why." She sounded very coherent, she thought proudly. "Most authorities think it became a tradition when the ancient Greek sailors honored the Goddess Athena."

"I hope I haven't offended your women's lib sensibilities," he drawled. "After all, it's a unisex name."

"Women's lib? What's that?"

He started to smile but it faded into incredulity. She wasn't joking; she actually didn't know. "I'll explain it to you later," he said slowly. Then his mischievous grin lit the lean darkness of his face. "Or then again maybe I won't!"

"Good heavens, it's enormous." Kate's eyes widened in disbelief, her gaze on the three-masted schooner berthed at the dock. "I saw a windjammer cruise ship docked in St. Thomas once and this is almost as large as that."

"I like to be comfortable," Beau said easily. "And I have guests occasionally."

"You must be very rich," Kate said soberly. "It's a beautiful ship, Beau."

"Stinking rich," he said inelegantly. "And I told you in the bar I'd be more than generous with you. You won't have to worry."

"I'm not worried." She glanced away so he wouldn't see how much his words had hurt. "You've been very generous already. If you'll just get Jeffrey away from Castellano, I promise I won't ask for anything else."

His hand was beneath her elbow helping her up the gangplank with a protectiveness that was very comforting. Now that she thought about it, that concern had been in evidence during the entire trip back to the ship from the warehouse. The walk had been made in almost total silence, but Beau's hand had been there to support her at every curb or sudden roughness in the cobblestone street. That instinctive care was yet another anomaly in the complexity of his personality.

"You may change your mind later," he said cynically. "I won't hold you to it. I'm used to paying for what I want. However, I'll see that you get that first installment right away." He gestured toward the man who was strolling lazily along the deck toward them. "Or, I should say, Daniel will. Daniel is very experienced in getting things done, aren't you, Daniel?"

"Very," the big man agreed amiably. "I know all the best ways of making bail, of finding the nearest emergency clinic in every port in the Caribbean, not to mention my talent for bribing or soothing irate fathers, brothers, and sundry municipal officials. What would you do without me, Beau?"

"He's also captain of the *Searcher* in his spare time," Beau said with a grin. "Sometimes he forgets to mention that. Daniel Seifert, Kate Gilbert. Kate's going to be with us for a while."

Daniel Seifert enclosed her hand in a gigantic paw with surprising gentleness. He was somewhere in his middle thirties and almost as large and brawny as Julio. There the resemblance ended. His trendily cut auburn hair, snapping dark blue eyes and trim auburn beard gave him an attractiveness that had a much more virile impact than Julio's dark good looks.

"I approve of you far more than I did the earlier arrivals," he said, his dark eyes twinkling. "We have enough men on this ship."

"Julio and Jeffrey arrived safely?" Kate asked, relieved.

Seifert nodded. "About an hour and a half ago. I quartered them with the crew." He lifted an inquiring brow at Beau. "Is that okay?"

"For now," Beau said with a shrug. "Are we ready to get under way?"

"As you command." Daniel's mocking smile

was a white slash in his bearded face. "Would I dare disobey?"

Beau snorted. "You'd dare do anything, if it pleased you." His glance fell to the captain's huge hand still clasping Kate's. "Are you going to let her have her hand back or are you hoping to form a permanent attachment?"

"The idea has definite merit." Seifert released her hand reluctantly. "I suppose you've already established a prior claim though."

"Definitely." The single word was crisp and incisive.

"Then I gather the guest cabin I had readied won't be needed," Seifert said lightly. "What a pity."

"I have to see Julio and Jeffrey and tell them I'm on board and safe," Kate said, biting her lip worriedly. "Julio won't be able to rest until I do."

Beau shook his head. "Not tonight. You can see them tomorrow morning." He turned to the captain. "I'm taking her to my cabin. Drop in and let Rodriguez know she's safe, will you?"

Seifert nodded. "Right away. I suppose it would be rudely inquisitive of me to ask what she's safe from?"

"I'll tell you later." Beau's hand on her elbow was propelling her forward. "You'll be sorry you missed it."

"Possibly," the captain drawled. "Your companions in deviltry aren't generally as charming as Miss Gilbert." He watched Beau open the door to the passage to the lower deck. "But haven't you forgotten something?"

Beau glanced over his shoulder impatiently. "What?"

"Where am I to get under way for? Trinidad?"

Beau shrugged. "Just get out of Costellano territorial waters PDQ. We'll decide our destination tomorrow."

THREE

THE MASTER CABIN was surprisingly large and luxurious for a sailing vessel. The bunk against the far wall was oversized and covered with a denim spread in a cheerful melon color that contrasted with the rich oak of the walls and the brown and beige tweed of the carpet. The built-in bookcase was enclosed with doors that were carved with a fretted openwork design that gave the modern room a pleasing touch of Mediterranean opulence.

"This is very nice," Kate said, her gaze lingering on the bookcase. "I can see what you mean by being comfortable." All those lovely books. The doors offered tempting glimpses of everything from leather-bound weighty-looking tomes to bright slick jacketed novels. What wouldn't she give for a week with that bookcase.

Then with a little sense of shock she realized she might very well have that week. That was why she was in this cabin. To make herself available to Beau Lantry in that bunk she'd been admiring so impersonally. Tonight. He'd said he wanted to consummate their bargain as soon as possible and brought her to his cabin for that purpose. Why wasn't she more nervous at the thought of that consummation with this total stranger? The only thing she seemed capable of feeling was this chilling weariness and lethargy that seemed to be seeping into every bone.

"I'm glad you like it," Beau said crisply. With his hand beneath her elbow, he steered her across the room toward the bed. "Since you'll be spending a good deal of time here in the future. Sit down." He gave her a nudge that reinforced the invitation that was more of a command and she found herself sitting on the edge of the bunk and gazing up at him wearily. His hands were on the buttons of her chambray shirt and he had three of them unbuttoned before she fully realized what he was doing. So soon? Evidently he was too impatient to wait any longer for his payment.

She looked up into his intent face bent close to her own. She didn't try to interfere with his deft disrobing of her. He was perfectly entitled to claim his rights to her body at any time he chose, she thought tiredly. She just wished he'd given her a chance to rest a little first. "If you don't mind, I'd like to take a shower before we do it," she said quietly. "It's been quite an evening in a number of ways."

His eyes flew up to meet her eyes and she saw a flicker of surprise in their depths. "Do 'it'?" There was a thread of barely repressed anger in his voice. "What the hell kind of men have you been sleeping with, for Lord's sake? Do they all jump your bones when you're so tired and hurt you're practically ready to pass out?"

She looked down at her half-opened shirt in confusion. "But then why—"

"I'm going to get you cleaned up and into bed," he interrupted harshly. "And not to 'do it,' blast it! But first I want to take a look at your head. That bastard clipped you pretty damn hard in spite of what you said. I wanted to examine it back at the warehouse, but I didn't think you'd let me without putting up a fight and that would have been worse for you than the walk back to the ship."

"There's nothing wrong with me. I told you . . ."

He finished unbuttoning the blue shirt and pushed it off her shoulders, his hand reaching around to unfasten her plain white bra with experienced skill. "Bull. I was a professional athlete too long not to recognize the signs. You were carrying yourself all the way back here as though you'd break apart at any minute."

"You were an athlete?" she repeated, surprised. "No wonder you looked so coordinated when you dove through that window."

"Well, I'm sorry to disappoint you, but I wasn't a circus acrobat as you thought," he said wryly. "I was a featured skater in an ice revue for a while and then a coach for an Olympic contender the next six years."

"And what do you do now?"

"At the moment I appear to be acting as a

combination lady's maid and ship's doctor," he said crisply as he lowered the bra straps over her arms. "But usually I'm a glorified bum. The glory resulting when you're properly endowed with filthy lucre."

"I see."

"Do you?" He glanced up, his eyes narrowed on her face. "No recriminations for being a worthless playboy, no attempts at reformation of my wicked dissolute ways?"

"I don't have any right to do that," she said gravely. "And you don't seem all that dissolute."

"Perhaps not in comparison with some of your companions," he agreed grimly. He pulled the bra away from her breasts and then froze. He inhaled sharply. "Liane was wrong. You're not thin at all." He reached out and touched one breast with a hesitant, gentle finger. "You're full and beautifully, perfectly round." His eyes darkened to a smoky hazel. "And so silky." His finger traced a circle about the dark pink nipple. "Golden silk. Lord, I've never seen such skin, warm and soft and silky as a small child's. The first time I saw you in the bar I wondered if you'd feel like this."

"Well, now you know," she said shakily. She felt as if that lazy finger were scorching and searing as it moved and suddenly she forgot about the weariness and throbbing ache in her temple. She moistened her lips. "Have you changed your mind?"

"No," he said thickly. "My mind is still as resolute as ever, it's my body that's undergoing all the changes. Are you this tan all over?"

She nodded. "I like the sun. There's a little pool in the rain forest where we keep the Cessna that I sunbathe next to sometimes."

His finger touched the perky pink tip. "Nude?" he asked huskily.

"Yes." She could barely get the word out. "There's never anyone around." Her throat was dry and tight and she was sure he could hear the beating of her heart caused by his gossamer light touch. She hadn't realized before how sensitive her body could be, how a tentative caress could send hot signals to her entire body. She didn't have to look down to realize that her nipple was budding and her breast flowering for him. She could see it in the darkening of Beau's eyes.

Strange, she felt as if all their responses were now curiously linked.

"I'm going to watch you do that someday," he said, his voice as velvet soft as his finger. "I'm going to sit and watch the sun pour down on you like golden rain, caressing you and making you glow." His thumb and index finger pinched gently and she felt an aching incompletion in her loins. "And then I'm going to come to you and make you glow for me. I want to feel you open and flower and tremble." She could see the wild cadence of the pulse beat in his temple. "I want to know that everything I do to you will make you shine and melt and flow." He drew a deep shuddering breath and shook his head as if to clear it. "I must be going crazy. For a minute I could actually see you lying there waiting for me to come to you." His hand dropped away and he stepped backward. "Come on, we'd better get you in the shower or I'm going to forget you're not fair game." He pulled her to her feet. "Get out of the rest of those clothes while I find something for you to put on." He strode to the built-in closet and slid back the door. "Tomorrow you'll have to make do with a pair of my shorts and a T-shirt while your own things are being laundered. Do you often have to make a run for it with only the clothes on your back?"

"No, this is the first time." She kicked off her tennis shoes and pulled off her jeans, her gaze fixed on his back as he riffled through the closet. "Actually, we don't move all that often. Jeffrey sets up operations and lets his clients come to him. We've been on Castellano for about four years."

"You make him sound like a corporate attorney," Beau drawled. "But from what I hear about Castellano, it must have been ideally suited to your friend's occupation." He pulled out an ice-blue satin negligee trimmed in fine Valenciennes lace. "I thought I remembered seeing this in there," he said, looking at it critically. "Barbara must have forgotten it when she left the ship at Barbados. The blue should be good with your eyes. Do you object to wearing another woman's clothes?"

Barbara? How many of his mistresses had occupied this cabin and why did the thought of those women hurt so much? "No, I don't mind," she said softly. "I'd be awfully ungrateful to be that petty, wouldn't I?"

"I'm glad you're so sensible. I know quite a few women who'd . . ." He glanced back over his shoulder and the words died away. She was totally naked and standing there gazing at him with clear unflinching honesty. No coyness, just the quiet serene acceptance that had so moved him before. There were dark circles beneath her eyes and weariness in the slight droop of her shoulders, but it didn't affect the valiant sturdiness of her stance. He must be getting old, he thought cynically, he'd never before looked at a lovely naked woman and only noticed how courageous she was. And she *was* lovely. Those beautiful full breasts flowed into the supple slenderness of her waist and hips and her long legs were strong and shapely. Her entire body was strong and graceful yet there was a fragility about her bone structure that gave her an air of intense vulnerability. Strength and vulnerability. The ambivalent physical mixture was echoed in her personality and he was finding it a very explosive combination, indeed. He glanced at the negligee in his hand and felt a sudden violent distaste he refused to examine too closely. He impulsively hung the robe back in the closet and pulled a white terry-cloth one of his own off its hanger.

"This will be more comfortable," he said tersely, sliding the closet door closed and tossing the robe on the bunk. "Come on." He opened the door to the adjacent bathroom and stepped into its brown and beige ceramic confines. He adjusted the water in the frosted shower stall to a warm soothing flow and stepped aside with a mockingly gallant gesture. "Mademoiselle. I'll join you in a moment as soon as I get out of these clothes." The frosted shower door closed between them.

She was glad the sudden hotness of her cheeks could be attributed to the steam that was rising from the water. It had been intimidating enough having him look at her for those long moments with that curiously enigmatic expression, but she hadn't imagined he'd be stripping and stepping into the tiny shower cubicle with her. There was scarcely room for one, much less two, beneath the spray. She drew a deep steadying breath and squared her chin. What earthly difference did it make? Now or later both minor and major intimacies would come at Beau Lantry's discretion. She'd better be prepared to accept that fact.

"Move a little forward, Kate." The frosted glass door was open and she instinctively obliged as Beau stepped into the shower and closed the door behind him. She could feel the warmth of his chest touching her back as he leaned forward to pick up the soap from the holder. "Let me get a little of this stench off of me and then I'll take care of you. Tossing garbage cans around and playing with gasoline and trash piles sure tests a man's deodorant." She could feel him moving behind her, occasionally touching her as he soaped his chest and torso, but she kept her gaze fixed rigidly on the ceramic wall in front of her. "Are you feeling all right? No dizziness or nausea?"

"No, I told you I was fine," she said quickly. Except for the way her heart was pounding as if it wanted to jump out of her breast. Except for her skin that was becoming so sensitive to the casual brush of his that it seemed to ache and burn with every touch. "He didn't hurt me."

"The hell he didn't." His hands were at her

waist as he shifted her a little to the side so that the full spray of water would hit him and rinse off the film of soap. "I should have cremated the bastard."

"You almost did," she said breathlessly. His hands hadn't lingered on her waist for more than an instant, yet she still felt them there. "For a second I was almost more afraid of you than I was of them."

"Afraid?" She could feel his gaze on her but her own remained riveted straight ahead. "You didn't give the impression of being frightened. If I recall, you wanted to bust in there and take them both on by yourself."

"That doesn't mean I wasn't afraid," she said simply. "It was just something that had to be done. You always have to do what has to be done even if you're not very brave. You simply block out everything and get it over with."

"Do you?" There was an odd note of tenderness in his voice. "Then, of course, I was mistaken. No red badge of courage for you."

"That was a wonderful book, wasn't it?" she asked eagerly, her face lighting up. "I found an English copy in a used bookstore in Maracaibo a few years ago. I can usually only find Spanish or Portuguese translations and I always think it's much nicer to read a book in the original, don't you?"

"Oh, indubitably," he drawled. "How many languages do you read?"

"Spanish and Portuguese," she answered. "I speak a little French, but I can't read or write it."

"What a shame," he said mildly. "Turn around here and let me take a look at that head." His hands were on her shoulders. "So you're a Stephen Crane fan. Who else do you like?"

"Everyone," she said with a dreamy smile as she obediently turned to face him. "Shakespeare, Samuel Clemens, Walter Scott." His hands were parting the short wet strands that were clinging seal-like around her face. "I particularly like Shakespeare. There's so much music in his words."

"You have something against the twentieth century?" He was probing gently at the swelling, his expression carefully impersonal.

"No, it's just easier to get hold of the classics in a foreign country."

"This doesn't seem too bad," he said, relieved.

"No headache?" His hands fell to her nape and began a gentle kneading massage of the tense muscles of her neck and shoulders.

"No." She found to her surprise that she was speaking the truth. The painful throbbing had all but disappeared and the combination of the soothing spray and those magical fingers was melting every muscle in her body into a state resembling warm butter. Unconsciously she nestled closer, laying her head on his chest like a contented child. "It's all gone."

"Good." She felt his lips brush her forehead. "Which Shakespearean play do you like best?"

"*Romeo and Juliet.* I know it's not considered his most cerebral, but there's something about it that touches me every time. And the words . . ." Her arms linked absently about his waist. "They're like sunlight, all clear and shining and beautiful."

"Golden rain?" he suggested. His thumb had found the cords of tension in the center of her nape with delicious accuracy.

"Um-hmm." She nodded, conscious of the damp thatch of hair beneath her cheek and the scent of soap and musk that surrounded him. "I never thought of it quite like that, but it's a lovely way to describe it. A golden rain of words." She moved a little closer. "I love the way—" She broke off as she felt the unmistakable evidence of his arousal pressing against her stomach. Her eyes widened in shock as they flew down his body.

He chuckled. "What did you expect? Those pretty nipples have been poking into me, and I've been dying to cuddle that pert little derriere since the instant I stepped in here. I'm not an iron man, you know."

She started to back away. "I'm s-sorry," she stammered in confusion. "I didn't mean—"

"Hush," he said softly. His hands on her nape tightened as he tilted her head up to meet his eyes. "I'm not an iron man but I'm not a boy either. Of course I want you, but I'm not going to throw you down on the floor and rape you. I can handle it." He cast a mischievous glance down at himself and his eyes were suddenly dancing. "As long as you promise you won't!"

A little smile tugged at her lips. The man was really outrageous. "I'll try to restrain myself."

She was standing here naked as the day she

was born actually joking with this impossibly attractive man, she thought in bewilderment. What was even more unusual was that after that first moment of excruciating shyness, she'd felt perfectly natural and relaxed about it. He was such a strange man. Tenderness and violence, mischief and cynicism, virile lust and almost maternal gentleness. Yet she felt as comfortable with him in this moment as if she'd known him for years.

"I trust you," he said airily, as he reached for the knob and turned off the water. "You've demonstrated an amazing amount of strength of will in other areas. But I still think I'd better get you out of here and away from temptation." He whisked her out of the shower stall and wrapped her carefully in a towel before turning away. "Run along into the cabin while I dry off. You'll find a hair dryer in the top drawer of the dresser and an electric outlet on the wall by the bunk." He patted her bottom through the terry cloth of the towel. "Be sure to put on that robe right away. The air conditioning in the cabin is turned up fairly high to combat the humidity."

"I'll do that," she said bemusedly as she

opened the bathroom door. His streak of possessive protectiveness was constantly catching her off guard and filling her with strange warmth. She was the one who'd always nurtured and protected. It felt very odd being on the receiving end after all these years. Odd . . . and rather nice.

She was sitting on the bunk, bundled up in the white terry robe and just finishing blow-drying her hair when he padded out of the bathroom. A towel was slung carelessly about his hips, but he was otherwise nude. His hair was still damp but he'd combed it into its former slightly rakish orderliness. Without clothes he looked like the athlete he claimed to be, she thought absently. There wasn't an inch of fat on that lean muscular torso and his legs and arms had a supple whipcord strength that was both symmetrical and graceful. He must have been beautiful when he was skating, she thought dreamily. She would have liked to have seen him then.

"Why did you quit skating?" she asked impulsively.

"I was through with it," he said as he crossed the cabin to stand in front of her. He reached out a hand as if to test the dampness of her hair, but paused to play with a curl, unwinding it and then allowing it to spring back into its former ringlet. "It was fun for a while but I've never been known for my stability. There's no use sticking around once something has lost its zing."

She felt a sudden inexplicable jab of pain somewhere near her heart. No, Beau Lantry would never be interested in permanence or stability. Even on such short acquaintance she should have known that. It was all there in the reckless curve of that beautiful sensual mouth and the flickering restlessness in his eyes.

"I like your hair," he said. "It's all soft silky fleece. You're silky all over, your skin, your hair. . . ." His hand dropped and he turned away. "You're dry enough. Climb into bed and I'll turn out the light."

She switched off the portable dryer and put it in his outstretched hand. "On which side do you prefer that I sleep, left or right?" she asked politely.

His lips quirked. "Under," he answered, "or over." Then as her brow knitted in confusion, his golden eyes twinkled. "Never mind. It was just a thought. Sleep next to the wall. It will give me the illusion that I have you trapped and helpless."

"You do have me trapped and helpless," she murmured as she pulled back the coverlet and slipped beneath it. "It's no illusion."

His smile faded. "That's right, I do." He strode across the room and tossed the dryer carelessly on the dresser. "How stupid of me to forget." His hand brushed the switch on the wall, plunging the room into darkness.

She watched his dark shadow come toward the bunk, pausing only to jerk the towel from around his hips. She felt the mattress give as he slipped into the bed beside her and she drew a deep breath trying to relax.

"Come here, Kate." He was scooting closer and drawing her into his arms with casual matter-of-factness. "I want to cuddle you." His hands were moving soothingly up and down her back. "You're stiff as a board, sugar." That faint Southern drawl was dark velvet as he pressed his face into the curls at her temple. "Just a cuddle, that's all. Relax and let me love you a little." His lips were teasing, pulling at one tight curl. "I love your hair. I keep wanting to run my hands through it and play like a little kid. What's it like when it's long?"

"Terrible," she said faintly. She could feel the heat of his naked flesh even through the thick terry of the robe. "It's so soft that it tangles at the first breeze. That's why I keep it short."

"Ummm." He rubbed his cheek back and forth against it in a gesture that was half sensual, half boyish. "I think I'd like it long. You'd look sort of wild and gypsyish," he said. "Though this is fine too."

"I'm glad you think so," she said dryly, "since I have no intention of letting it grow."

"We'll see," he said absently. His hands were plucking discontentedly at the back of the terry robe. "This thing is damnably rough. I want to get at you." Then he sighed and drew her closer into the curve of his arm, settling her head in the hollow of his shoulder. "You're tired, right? And if I'm not going to be on the same level as that bastard who tried to clobber you, I've got to remember, right? Go to sleep, Kate."

"If you'd rather—"

"'Do it'?" he interrupted. "Oh, yes, I definitely

would. But every now and then I find myself overcome by the code of chivalrous Southern manhood." His tone was distinctly testy. "At the most fiendishly inconvenient times."

"I owe you a—"

"Kate, sweet Kate, shut up." His hand was combing through her curls. "I'm quite aware you're ready to lay that silky body on the line and it isn't making it any easier for me."

"Okay," she whispered. The events of the evening, together with the emotional upheavals she'd undergone, were catching up with her and she almost collapsed against him. Her voice was a little slurred with exhaustion. "If it's all right with you?"

"It will have to be."

Suddenly out of the mists of sleep rapidly enfolding her a fragmentary memory drifted to her. "Who is Uncle George?"

"What?"

"Uncle George," she murmured. "You said Despard reminded you of Uncle George."

"Oh, no one important. Just one of my more avaricious relatives. I hadn't thought of the old bastard for years before I ran into Despard."

There was a long silence and she was half asleep when Beau began to chuckle. "Lord, if only Daniel could see me now."

"Daniel?" she asked drowsily.

"He'd never believe it." There was amusement vying with the exasperation in his tone. "Discussing Shakespeare and Samuel Clemens with a naked woman in the shower and then lying in bed pure as the driven snow with that same woman. He'd enjoy the entire episode tremendously."

"Would he?" She could barely keep her eyes open. "You're very good friends, aren't you?"

"We've been in a few tight spots together. It has a tendency to breed a certain intimacy."

"He's such a strange-looking man. Not at all like any picture I've ever seen of Charon."

"Charon?"

"The ferryman," she muttered, burrowing her head deeper into his shoulder. "Over the River Styx."

"Oh, that Charon." Beau's velvet drawl hinted at repressed laughter. "Forgive me for not making the connection. I can see how the territorial waters of Castellano would remind you of the river of the dead under the present circumstances, but I'm afraid Daniel wouldn't be flattered to be compared to that particular mythical figure." One lazy finger was winding itself around a silky curl. "He was a ferocious old graybeard as I recall."

"Well, the beard was right anyway." Her eyes refused to stay open any longer.

"You seem to be really hung up on mythology. Did you study it in school?"

She shook her head. "I never went to school," she said sleepily. "I read about it in my encyclopedia."

His voice was deceptively casual. "You never went to school?"

"Well, at least not after I was seven years old. We moved around too much." She wished he'd quit asking questions. She just wanted to go to sleep. "But Jeffrey said it didn't really matter. When I was eight, he bought me a set of encyclopedias and had me study fifteen pages a day until I'd gone through all of them. He said that was as good as any stuffy old school."

"Oh, he did?" The amusement was completely gone and he sounded almost grim. "Your Jeffrey seems to have all sorts of peculiar theories about what's good for you." It wasn't any wonder, he thought, that she wasn't like anyone he'd ever met before. "Do you always do what he tells you?"

But she was already asleep, her breathing deep and steady as she curled trustfully into the curve of his arm.

A set of encyclopedias, for heaven's sake! Mythology and the classics and millions of facts without interpretation. And a young girl with an insatiable hunger for the printed word, eagerly devouring those facts and reaching for more. Then another thought occurred to him. Women's lib. She hadn't known about women's lib.

He found himself shaking her awake. "Those encyclopedias, Kate. What year were they published?"

"What?" she asked groggily.

"The year they were published," he demanded.

"Oh, that," she muttered, "1960." Then she was once more asleep.

He slowly settled back down on the pillow, his

eyes staring blankly into the darkness. "Well, I'll be damned!"

Jeffrey Brenden was leaning on the rail of the ship, his curly gray-streaked hair ruffled by the brisk morning breeze. In the oversized jeans and gray sweatshirt he'd obviously borrowed from a member of the crew his slight wiry frame appeared even more slender than it had last night. However, his brown eyes were shrewd and alert as he glanced up as Beau approached.

"Ah, my generous host, I assume." He stretched out his hand, his grin warm and genial. "Julio tells me I have a great deal to thank you for." He made a face. "I'm afraid I don't remember. It seems I was more than a little sloshed last night."

"More than a little," Beau agreed dryly. He glanced around the empty deck. "Where's your friend Rodriguez?"

"He and the captain are having breakfast with the crew." Brenden's lips twisted ruefully. "I wasn't up to even staring a cup of coffee in the face this morning." His eyes traveled wistfully over the tall masts. "This is a beautiful ship, Mr. Lantry. I've always wanted to own a sailing ship."

"Why didn't you buy one?" Beau asked caustically. "According to Kate, it would have fit your image a hell of a lot better than a plane. She says you're something of a modern Sir Francis Drake."

"I'm a smuggler," Brenden said simply. "Kate always lets me justify it with that romantic nonsense, but I know what I am." He smiled a little sadly. "Lately it's been difficult to ignore. Despard's been rubbing my nose in it."

"And Kate's," Beau said deliberately. "Do you think it's fair to involve her in your illicit enterprises?"

"Kate's never been involved," Brenden said defensively. "I've always kept her out of it."

"You might have difficulty in convincing the authorities of that. She could be considered an accomplice, you know." His lips tightened. "And it's obvious you'd have trouble keeping her from involving herself, if last night is anything to go by."

There was a touch of fond pride mixed with

ruefulness in Brenden's smile. "You're right. She's a determined little monkey when she makes up her mind to do something. She always plunges headlong into the fray and to hell with the consequences." His eyes were full of memories. "I remember even when she was a child, she was like a little mother. She used to tell me, 'Don't worry, Jeffrey, it will all work out. *I'll* make it work.'" He turned around, leaning his elbows on the rail. "And do you know something? Most of the time she'd actually do it."

"You've known each other a long time," Beau observed. "She said you were friends. How did you get together?"

"Her mother was an American showgirl in a nightclub in Rio de Janeiro." He shrugged. "We lived together for a year or so. Then Sally decided to move on to greener pastures. She just packed up and left one day while I was in Santiago." He paused. "She left Kate behind."

"Charming," Beau grated through clenched teeth. He felt the same surge of savagery he'd known last night when he'd seen that bastard hit Kate with the pistol. "She just forgot about her, I suppose. Like an old pair of shoes."

"Sally wasn't all that bad," Brenden said quietly. "She just wasn't the maternal type. She didn't know how to cope with a seven-year-old." He grimaced. "Neither did I."

"So you didn't bother," Beau said grimly. "You just dragged her along with you over half the Southern Hemisphere into every dive and hellhole."

"Would you rather I'd left her on her own in a foreign country?" Brenden asked. "At least she had a roof over her head." He met Beau's eyes steadily. "I never tried to be a father to her, but I did the best I could. We got along."

"For God's sake, you didn't even send her to school!"

"There were reasons." Brenden looked away evasively. "Kate's sharp as a whip. She probably knows more than any of those fancy college graduates."

"I don't doubt it as long as the subject matter is pre-1960," Beau bit out. "But what about everything that's happened in her own lifetime? The space age, the Vietnam war, women's lib, Kennedy's assassination?"

"She picked up a lot of that on her own,"

Brenden said defensively. "And the rest isn't all that important for her to know."

"Did you tell her she didn't miss much there either?" Beau laughed incredulously. "I bet you did. And what's worse, she probably believed you."

"I did the best I could," the older man repeated stubbornly. His expression turned sulky. "And why the hell is it any of your business anyway? You did us a favor but that doesn't make you Kate's keeper."

"She obviously needs one," Beau said curtly. "You haven't even asked where Kate is, or don't you really give a damn?"

Brenden went still. "I give a damn." His eyes narrowed on Beau's face. "Where is Kate?"

"When I left her, she was curled up asleep." Beau paused deliberately. "In my bed."

There was a flicker on Brenden's face that might have been pain and then it became totally impassive. "I see."

"Is that all you've got to say?" Beau could feel the fury blazing up in him and made a futile effort to control it. "Is it such a common occurrence that you don't even raise an eyebrow? Aren't you even going to ask if I enjoyed her?"

"No, I'm not going to ask you that," Brenden said heavily, turning back to stare out to sea. "That's between the two of you. It's none of my business."

"Funny, I thought it was very much your business. Kate was willing to throw herself into my bed to bail the three of you out of the mess you'd gotten yourselves into. Evidently that kind of commitment only goes one way."

Brenden was silent, his gaze fixed on the horizon.

Beau drew a deep breath. "I don't know what the devil I'm getting so hot about. If her so-called friends don't care that she's willing to make a prostitute of herself, why should I?" But he *did* care and the fact that it did matter made him even angrier.

Brenden's glance was glacier cold. "Kate's *not* a prostitute. Before you throw that first stone, you might consider you were willing enough to take advantage of her generosity yourself and no doubt will again at the next opportunity. Julio's been having a chat with the crew and what he heard about your way with women doesn't make you sound like an angel."

"I never claimed to be a celibate," Beau said, his eyes smoldering. "But I'm no pimp either."

"And neither am I," Brenden snapped back, obviously stung. "If I'd been myself I would never have let her do it."

"But you're not rushing down to my cabin to pull her out of my lecherous clutches," Beau said sarcastically. "You seem amazingly complacent about the whole business."

"Not complacent," Brenden said, his voice heavy with weariness. "But for once in my life I'm trying to be practical. What's done is done. It's up to Kate if she wants to stay where she is. If she doesn't, I'll find a way to help her."

"It's not likely she'd make that choice, once she'd made a bargain," Beau said with a sardonic smile. "Even I know her well enough to know that and you sure as hell should."

"Yes, I know that." Brenden's eyes met his. "And perhaps it's just as well in the long run."

"For you?"

Brenden shook his head. "For her." He smiled

sadly. "You've just taken pains to tell me what a lousy protector I've been. Maybe it's time I let somebody else have a shot at it."

"You're absolutely astonishing," Beau said blankly. "You've never seen me before in your life, yet you're willing to trust Kate to me. What's to prevent me from using her any way I please and then kicking her off the ship at the next port?"

"Nothing," Brenden said. "Except for the fact that since the minute you saw me, you've been reading me the riot act for treating her so badly. It doesn't seem likely you'd do that and then go off and do the same thing yourself." He shrugged. "And when you get tired of her, I think you'll be generous. You're obviously a very rich man from what Julio gathered. You'll see she's secure until she is able to take care of herself."

"You're speaking as if I'm some Regency buck offering an obliging mistress carte blanche." Beau shook his head dazedly. "Kate was right. You're something from the eighteenth century."

"It takes one to know one." Brenden's brown eyes were narrowed and shrewd. "I think you may be something of a throwback yourself, Mr. Lantry. There aren't many men who wander around the Caribbean on a sailing ship entangling themselves in situations like the one at Alvarez's last night."

"Don't depend on it."

"I learned a long time ago not to depend on anything," Brenden said. "But I still find it difficult not to hope." He suddenly looked much older. "Particularly when it comes to Kate. She's always given so much to everyone. I'd like to think that there's justice somewhere in this god-awful world." His hands closed tightly on the rail. "She sure won't get it as long as she sticks with me. She could have gotten herself killed last night. Despard doesn't play around, he goes straight for the jugular."

Beau tried to hold on to his anger. Damn it, he would *not* be sorry for the appealing old reprobate. "I doubt if it's the first time. Why this sudden attack of conscience?"

"Maybe I'm getting too old to fool myself anymore," Brenden said. "Time has a way of fraying our illusions around the edges." His lips twisted. "It has a habit of transforming dashing pirates into shabby petty criminals. Anyway, I've decided to opt out of the dreams game," he said gloomily. "I'm going to reform."

Beau's eyes narrowed suspiciously on the other man's face. "Reform?"

Brenden nodded. "There's a nice little widow who owns a coffee plantation on Santa Isabella, an island not too far from here. I've been keeping company with her off and on for the past five years." His mouth curved in a rueful grin. "She doesn't understand about pirates and smugglers either. A very practical lady, Marianna." His face softened. "But loving, very loving. I think I'll just have you drop me off at Santa Isabella and see if she's still interested in a more permanent relationship."

"And what about your friend Julio?"

He shook his head. "He'd never leave Kate. He puts up with me, but Kate makes his world go around. It's been that way since she yanked him out of the guerrilla army four years ago in El Salvador."

"Guerrilla army?" Beau asked. "She said he was eighteen now. That would have made him only fourteen."

Brenden nodded. "The guerrillas raid the villages and round up all the able-bodied males and 'draft' them into the army." His lips tightened grimly. "Some of them aren't over eleven or twelve years old. The other side is almost as bad. Julio was a big strapping kid even then, so he was a prime candidate. He'd been running errands and doing the shopping and cooking for us for about three months and Kate took a real liking to him. She was almost wild when she heard what happened to him."

"So she went after him." It was a statement, not a question. It was the kind of impulsive action Kate would inevitably take.

"*We* went after him," Brenden said. "And almost lost our scalps in the process. We ended up taking off in a hail of machine-gun bullets. Kate was afraid the civil authorities would try the same thing so she wouldn't even let us stay in the country." He shook his head. "Pity. I had to scratch the caper I was putting together."

"How unfortunate," Beau said ironically. "I imagine revolution-torn countries are very conducive to your line of work."

"They are rather," Brenden agreed. "All that

turmoil . . ." He trailed off and straightened briskly. "Well, I'd better hunt up Captain Seifert and ask him to set course for Santa Isabella. He says we're just outside Castellano territorial waters so it shouldn't take more than a few hours to reach there." He arched an eyebrow. "With your permission, of course."

Beau nodded curtly. "I said I'd take you wherever you wanted to go. It was part of the bargain."

Brenden flushed. "Ah, yes, the bargain. Well, at least you appear to be a man who keeps his promises." He started to walk away, then paused, his wistful gaze returning to the wild free beauty of the billowing sails. For a moment his expression once again revealed that he was full of the dreams he'd said he'd abandoned. "Did you know that John Hancock was rumored to be a smuggler, Mr. Lantry?"

FOUR

KATE COULD FEEL her eyes sting and burn with unshed tears but she blinked them determinedly away. Jeffrey looked so lonely despite the jaunty set of his shoulders as he jumped lightly out of the dinghy and strode rapidly up the pier away from them. She waited until he'd rounded the corner at the end of the dock before she turned to Beau, who was standing beside her at the rail of the *Searcher*. "He's going to have problems, you know," she said huskily. "He thinks he's going to be able to settle down, but it's going to chafe at him terribly."

"You were talking to him a long time on the

way here," Beau observed. "Don't tell me you were trying to talk him out of his change of lifestyle?"

"Of course not," Kate said, frowning. "Marianna's a wonderful woman and she'll take terrific care of Jeffrey. He should have done this years ago."

"Then what's the problem?"

"Jeffrey's always been so independent." She bit her lip worriedly. "He's not going to like feeling he's beholden to Marianna for an income." Her chin squared determinedly. "I'm going to have to do something about that."

"Why do I suddenly have a nasty chill down my spine?" Beau asked warily. "May I ask what you're intending to do?"

"I just can't let Jeffrey walk away without knowing he's going to be happy." How was she going to convince Beau? She'd thought that once he'd met Jeffrey he'd be more sympathetic toward her old friend. Most people liked Jeffrey even if they didn't approve of him. Beau, however, had displayed a very puzzling coldness and resentment toward him. "He's a very proud man."

"And?"

"A year or so ago he was talking about opening an interisland charter service. It never came to anything, but it's really just the kind of thing Jeffrey would be good at. He's a very good pilot and can land on a dime in all kinds of rough country."

"I can see where he'd gain a certain amount of expertise in that area," Beau said with an ironic smile. "What is all this leading up to?"

"Santa Isabella would be a perfect base of operations for a charter service. Besides the wealthy plantation owners there's a plush hotel and resort that opened recently on the other side of the island." She rushed on. "There's only one difficulty. We had to leave the Cessna on Castellano. I'll have to go back and get it."

"What!"

Oh dear, his face was darkening more by the second. "He needs the plane to start a charter service. I'll have to ferry it from Castellano to Marianna's coffee plantation." She was speaking rapidly, careful not to look at him. "It shouldn't take long. You can drop me off and then sail back here to Santa Isabella. As soon as

I've delivered the plane, I'll come directly to the pier and you can send the dinghy for me."

"Oh, I can?" Beau asked with deceptive calmness. "You have it all planned out. I take it you can fly a plane and land it on a dime as well as Jeffrey can?"

"I'm pretty good," she admitted. "Not as good as he is, of course, but I've been flying since I was fourteen. Julio's only been flying for the last two years and he's amazingly competent for the number of hours he's logged," she explained earnestly. "Jeffrey never let us become involved in any of his jobs, but we sometimes had to ferry the Cessna from one place to another."

"If he was often in the state he was in last night, I can see the reason why," Beau said grimly.

"Jeffrey didn't use to drink like that," Kate protested. "It's only lately that he's been—"

"I couldn't care less about your friend's drinking habits." Beau was holding on to his patience with no little effort. "Nor Julio's dazzling expertise in the cockpit. I'm wholly concerned with this insanity of yours about going back to Castellano."

"It's not insane, it's essential," Kate said stubbornly. "Jeffrey's going to need that plane and it's really my fault he doesn't have it. I should have thought of a way of getting us off the island in the Cessna to begin with." She sighed. "You're right. I'm too impulsive. I should have planned it all out ahead of time."

"And this isn't impulsive?" Beau exploded, his eyes blazing. "My Lord, you've just destroyed millions of dollars' worth of Despard's drugs in addition to bashing him on the head with a bourbon bottle. You say he's hand in glove with the government of Castellano, so if by any chance he doesn't get you, the authorities would be sure to. Yet you calmly tell me you're going to walk back there and retrieve a piece of misplaced property? You're damned right it's crazy!"

"Don't worry, I'm not going to involve you this time," she said soothingly. "All you have to do is drop me off in Castellano and then pick me up in Santa Isabella." She met his eyes gravely. "I'm not trying to back out of our agreement. I just have to do this first."

"I'm well aware you'd probably cut your

throat rather than break your promise," he said through his teeth. "And you don't need to worry about 'protecting' me. You may have this need to be a little mother to Brenden and the whole world, but just leave me out of it. I can take care of myself." He drew a deep breath. "And I can take care of you too. Since no one else seems capable of the job, I'm obviously elected. There's no way I'm going to take you back to Mariba. It would be sheer suicide to turn you loose on the streets."

"It's not going to be all that dangerous," she argued desperately. "Look, I'm not asking you to sail right into Mariba harbor. The plane is hidden clear on the other side of the island. That side is almost uninhabited. It's all rain forest and a few fishing villages along the lagoon. We have the Cessna stashed and camouflaged in a glade in the forest." She made a face. "On an island like Castellano, it was best no one knew its location. It's right on the main drug routes and planes and yachts are prime hijack targets. We keep it gassed and ready to go, so I can be in the air in less than an hour after I hit the beach. It will all be perfectly safe."

"If it's so perfectly safe, why don't we drop Julio off and let him ferry it?" Beau asked silkily. "You've just been telling me what a hotshot pilot he is."

Darn, she'd been afraid he'd ask that. "Well, there's a slight possibility Despard may have ordered an island-wide search for the plane," she admitted reluctantly. "He's bound to have discovered who you are by now. There aren't that many Americans who dock at Mariba. He'll put two and two together and realize we left Castellano by ship. Which leaves a very valuable commodity in the form of the Cessna just sitting there unguarded." She paused. "If he can find it."

"So you don't want to risk Julio but you're willing to put your own neck on the block." His voice was rough with impatience. "Do you have some kind of death wish or something?"

"This isn't Julio's responsibility," she said stubbornly. "It's mine. Jeffrey's my friend and he needs my help." Her eyes met his steadily. "He helped me when I needed him. I owe him."

The anger faded from his face but the exasperation remained. "A debt." He muttered a very explicit curse. "Why the hell did it have to be a debt?" He turned to the captain, who was leaning on the rail some distance down the deck talking casually to one of the seamen. "Daniel," he roared. "As soon as that blasted dinghy gets back, set sail for Castellano!"

Seifert's navy blue eyes showed no surprise as he straightened and turned to look at them. "Again?" he asked laconically. "I may not even have to use a navigation map this time."

"Very amusing," Beau said. He turned back to Kate. "I trust your Cessna has instruments. It will be almost sunset by the time we get back to Castellano and I want us to be off that island in one hour flat."

"Us? But I told you—"

"Us," he repeated with emphasis, his eyes flickering dangerously. "And if I were you, I wouldn't argue. At the moment I'm feeling a bit hot under the collar, to put it mildly. I'm within an inch of saying to hell with it and telling Daniel to head for Trinidad."

"The Cessna has instruments," she said absently, her curious gaze on Beau's irritated face. "Why *didn't* you tell Daniel to do that?"

"Because you hit me where I'm most vulnerable," Beau said tersely. "I believe in the payment of debts, damn it." He turned away. "And now I believe I'll go volunteer my help in getting under way again. I could use a little hard physical labor to work the edge off this temper." He was striding away from her toward the captain. "There are times when I wish to hell I still drank like a fish!"

"We should be sighting that lagoon you told us about in ten minutes or so." Daniel Seifert's deep voice was lazy as he paused beside her. "And so far no sign of the Castellano version of the Coast Guard. We just may make it after all."

Kate glanced up at him from where she was sitting on the hatch. The red-haired giant looked even more like a pirate the way he was dressed— in khaki shorts and rubber-soled tennis shoes, his massive bronze chest bared to the waist. "You don't seem too concerned," she said curiously. "Are you so used to dodging the authorities?"

His eyes twinkled as he looked down at her.

"Well, let's just say I have a limited experience in the field. I wasn't always the captain of a rich man's pleasure barge."

"No, I wouldn't think so," Kate said slowly. There was a charged vitality beneath that carelessly debonair exterior. "So why are you one now?"

He shrugged and dropped down beside her, crossing his iron-thewed legs tailor fashion. There was a long jagged scar on his left thigh and it only added to the barbaric wildness of his appearance. He saw her gaze upon it before she could glance away and ran his finger down it lightly. "Not very pretty, is it?" he asked with a grimace. "Well, what could you expect? I'd never stitched up anything in my life before."

"You sewed it yourself?" Kate's eyes widened in surprise.

"Well, no one else was going to do it. I was locked up in a dirty sod shack in the middle of the desert. I figured if I didn't close it up, I'd probably get blood poisoning before Clancy could haul me out of there. I had a hard time persuading those bastards to give me a needle and thread." His lips tightened. "I was right. I stayed in that six-by-four hotbox of a room for over six months."

She was staring at him in fascination. Daniel Seifert was obviously a very colorful man in more ways than the obvious. "That must have been terrible. Where was this desert? Did your friend, Clancy, finally break you out?"

"Sedikhan," Seifert said tersely. "And Clancy Donahue isn't my friend, he's my boss. He's head of security of the sheikdom of Sedikhan." His teeth flashed in a slightly tigerish grin. "And yes, he got me out, cleaned up the area—and the revolutionaries who put me in the shack. Very tidily, if somewhat lethally. Clancy is a very dangerous man, and very protective of his people."

"You're speaking present tense," Kate observed. "I thought Beau was your employer now."

He blinked in surprise. "I guess he is. Somehow I never thought of it like that. We just sort of flowed together some time ago and have been wandering around the Caribbean ever since." He drew up his knees and linked his arms loosely around them. "I always knew I'd go back to Sedikhan when I was ready. It was just a matter of time."

"I think you're better off doing what you're doing now," Kate said skeptically. "Your Mr. Donahue doesn't sound like he provides very safe working conditions."

Seifert chuckled. "You're right there, but then neither does Beau. I like a bit of excitement now and then. Maybe that's why I haven't been too eager to get back to Sedikhan even though I'm well now. Beau can provide almost as many fireworks as Clancy upon occasion."

"You were ill?" She glanced down at the scar. "Oh, of course, your leg."

He shook his head. "The leg healed pretty well. It was almost as good as new by the time Clancy rescued me." His loosely linked hands locked with unconscious tension. "It was my nerves that were shot. Six months in that hellhole only a little bigger than a coffin nearly drove me up the wall. Clancy could see I was in no kind of shape to keep on with our particular line of work, so he filled my bank account with enough cash to choke a horse and told me to go for a rest cure. Preferably somewhere without four surrounding walls." His eyes were narrowed on the horizon. "I'd captained one of Ben

Raschid's yachts a few years before and I knew where I'd find my place with no walls." He drew a deep breath of warm salt air. "And, Lord, I needed that place."

"But you're well now," she said gently. She supposed his frankness regarding his violent past should have repelled her but somehow it didn't. There was an oddly comforting strength and simplicity about this huge red-haired man. "And you don't have to go back to Sedikhan unless you want to."

"But I want to." He suddenly relaxed and the grin he gave her was lazily mocking. "Why not? Besides the amusement value, Donahue's lieutenants become very wealthy men in an amazingly short time. Living with Beau I've developed a taste for the kind of power money brings."

"I don't see how you could, living at sea on a ship like this," Kate said. "Surely life is very simple and uncomplicated."

"Don't kid yourself." The captain's lips twisted. "On the high seas we may be back to basic values, but once we hit port all the material values swing into focus. The Lantry conglomerate is one of the most powerful in the world. All

Beau has to do is to step ashore and the bowing and scraping starts. Maybe that's why he keeps such a low profile."

"A low profile?" Kate echoed blankly. "I didn't notice he was shy or retiring." She had a mental image of him tumbling through that warehouse window, a blazing torch in either hand. "Quite the contrary."

Seifert grinned. "Maybe I should say he keeps a low profile where society and government types are concerned. You're right, he's far from shy. You couldn't expect him to be. He was one of the most publicized orphans in the world, with all kinds of custody suits flying around him. He knew from the time he was out of diapers just how valuable he was to the world." His lips curved cynically. "Or how valuable his money was to it."

"I'd think that would make anyone a little spoiled."

"Beau's not spoiled," Seifert said, his smile fading. "You don't know him at all if you think that. I'm not saying he can't be self-indulgent on occasion, but all of us are guilty of that. He may do what he damn well pleases, but if there's a price, he's always willing to pay it." His expression was serious. "And I'm not just talking about cash. Growing up with that kind of money doesn't guarantee to make things easy. Did you know that Beau was an alcoholic?"

"No!" Her voice was as shocked as her face.

"He licked it several years ago but you don't go through something like that and stay an immature kid. He's tough as hell under that playboy façade."

"No wonder you get along so well." Kate's blue eyes were twinkling. "Like to like."

"Well, we did discover we had a certain affinity," he admitted with a slight smile. "We were both betwixt and between, so to speak. And we were both searching for something." His gaze was narrowed on the horizon again. "I knew what I was searching for: rest, peace, maybe even sanity, but I don't think Beau even knew he *was* searching."

"The *Searcher*," Kate mused. "This ship is named the *Searcher*."

Seifert nodded. "I renamed it. Beau had just bought it when we got together in Miami. He left it up to me to give it a new name. He didn't care what I called it as long as it wasn't the name of one of his past mistresses." His eyes glinted mischievously. "He didn't want any of them to think he had any lingering passion for them. I believe he had an expensive enough time getting rid of the ladies in the first place."

"I imagine he did." Kate remembered with a sharp pang Beau's remark about allowing her to change her mind later about the compensation she wanted from him. How many experiences with avaricious women had developed that bitter cynicism in him?

Seifert shrugged. "Well, anyway, he didn't care one way or the other, so it became the *Searcher*." His expression grew thoughtful. "I've often wondered if maybe that was what Beau was subconsciously looking for. Something that really mattered to him, something he could give a damn about."

Kate shook her head with a smile. "I can't say that I've noticed any lack of intensity in him." She wrinkled her nose. "Nor any lack of emotion. At the moment I have the impression he'd like to channel that intensity in my direction with some violence."

"I noticed he was a tad irritated," Seifert drawled. "I was a little surprised. Ordinarily he'd be looking forward to playing hide and seek with your local racketeers. It would be just the kind of thing he'd choose to while away a balmy tropic evening."

"Well," Kate said gloomily, "he didn't seem to find the idea one bit amusing."

"No, he didn't." The captain's gaze was suddenly fixed on her in speculation. "He was as furious as a speared shark and I think maybe a little worried. The latter is even more unusual. Beau regards worrying about the future as a sheer waste of time. Interesting."

"I'm glad you think so." Kate sighed. "I'd much rather he'd let me go in alone if he's so displeased with the entire idea."

"I just bet you would." Beau's tone was sour as he appeared suddenly beside them. He was also shirtless and his supple muscles gleamed golden in the lengthening rays of the setting sun. "You'd get a kick out of acting the big bold adventuress. How long do you think your luck is going to last pulling stunts like the one in Alvarez's saloon last night? If Despard ever gets

his hands on you, he'll probably murder you."
His lips tightened grimly. "After allotting a suitable amount of recreational time for gang rape."

"I'm not doing it to get some kind of cheap thrill," she said hotly. "You know I had—"

"All I know is that you're going back to that island and risking getting killed for a damn airplane," he interrupted harshly, his hazel eyes glinting gold. "I'll buy you a blasted Cessna if that's what you want. Hell, I'll buy you a Lear jet. Call it a fringe benefit."

The aching pain was raw and fierce and she looked away so that he couldn't see the liquid brightness in her eyes. "I told you I didn't want any of those," she said huskily. "I just want to get back Jeffrey's plane for him."

Beau muttered something violently obscene and Daniel gave a low surprised whistle.

"Then by all means let's go ashore and retrieve dear Jeffrey's property," Beau said with bitter savagery. He turned to Daniel. "I don't suppose you've noticed since you've been lolling on your duff passing the time of day with Kate, but we've come close enough to shore to launch the dinghy, if it wouldn't be too much trouble, that is."

"No trouble at all," the captain said genially, rising lazily to his feet. "Always willing to oblige, Beau."

Beau snorted inelegantly. "When it suits your convenience."

"Well, that goes without saying," Seifert said, his eyes twinkling. "Isn't it lucky it does in this case?" He sauntered off with surprising grace for so large a man.

He was only a few yards away when he halted in his tracks, his eyes on the horizon. This time his low whistle was sharp with startled apprehension. "I think we'd better forget the dinghy for the time being. I believe we're going to have visitors."

Kate jumped to her feet, her heart pounding in alarm. Her gaze followed Seifert's and she inhaled sharply. A launch painted a drab army green was headed in their direction.

"The local marines, I take it," the captain murmured. He glanced at Beau. "Do you want me to try to run for it?"

"Do we have a chance?"

"Not much." Daniel was observing the launch's approach with keenly analytical eyes.

Beau shrugged. "Then we'll let them board us. The most they can do is impound the ship and the conglomerate will be able to handle that. It will only be a matter of time."

"Julio!" Kate's frantic call brought the Latin boy dashing from the far end of the ship toward her. "Julio, hurry!" She was running for the rail facing the shore. With any luck the masts would hide them from being spotted through binoculars. Julio was beside her now, his face mirroring the same tension as her own. "They don't have a chance of outrunning it," she said tersely, pulling off her tennis shoes. "They're going to let the *Searcher* be boarded."

Julio muttered a curse and began to take off his own shoes.

Beau and Daniel were at their sides and Beau's face was dark as thunder. "What the hell do you think you're doing now?" he growled. "There's nothing to be afraid of. No matter how much clout Despard has with the government, I can protect you there. The conglomerate can buy and sell Castellano."

"He's right, Kate," the captain inserted swiftly. "I've seen it happen before. All Beau has to do is exert some economic muscle and we're home free."

"*You're* home free," Kate said grimly. She was climbing over the rail. "It will be easy for them to pull you out of their bureaucratic clutches. It wouldn't be so simple for Julio and me." She tried to smile reassuringly into Seifert's worried face. "Don't worry, we're not that far from shore and we're both very good swimmers. Jump, Julio!"

The boy slipped over the rail and dropped into the sea like a stone. Kate drew a deep breath and was about to release the rail herself, when Beau grabbed her roughly by the shoulders. "No! This is crazy. I tell you you're both perfectly safe, blast it! I can protect you."

"You think you can." Kate was struggling frantically. "Let me go! Do you know what happens to women who are imprisoned in Castellano? That gang rape you mentioned would be short and sweet in comparison."

"They wouldn't touch you," Beau said fiercely. "I wouldn't let them."

"You couldn't stop them," Kate cried, her eyes blazing. "That blanket of protection you're so smug about doesn't work for people like Julio and me."

"Why the hell not?"

"Because we don't have a country to back us up. They'll just lock us up and throw away the key." He was still looking at her with that expression of incomprehension and the launch was getting closer every second. "Because neither of us has a passport, damn it!"

"What?" Beau's grip loosened and she tore free and tumbled backward into the sea.

"No passport! How the hell can anyone go wandering around the world without a damned passport?" Beau asked furiously, jerking his shoes off and slipping over the rail. Julio's and Kate's heads were bobbing several yards from the ship as they struck out strongly for the shore. "I suppose I should have expected it. There isn't one single ordinary or reasonable thing connected with the woman!"

"Since when has the ordinary or reasonable appealed to you?" Daniel asked, raising a brow. "I gather you're going dashing . . . er, swimming, after her?"

"What the hell else can I do?" Beau asked

testily. "There's no telling what trouble she'll get into next. My God, no passport!"

"Any instructions, or do I play it by ear with the authorities?"

"Cover for us," Beau said tersely. "Tell them you let the four of us off at Santa Isabella and stick to it. I'll try to get in touch with you before the conglomerate pulls you out of Castellano, but if I don't, take the ship to Santa Isabella and we'll join you there."

"Right," Daniel said, scooping up the litter of shoes on the deck and tossing them overboard. "Wouldn't want to leave any evidence lying around when we're boarded, now would we? Have a pleasant swim, Beau."

"Thanks a lot," Beau said ironically, and dove into the sea.

FIVE

THE WATER HAD felt cold at first but now it was like warm satin flowing over her. She could see Julio's gleaming dark hair a few yards ahead and the shore seemed miles away. She felt a shiver of apprehension run through her. Would they be able to make it?

She bit her lip and struck out more determinedly. She mustn't even think there was a possibility of their not reaching the shore. She'd discovered a long time ago that doubts could be your worst enemy when you were striving to reach a goal. She blocked out everything but the rhythmic movement of her arms and legs that were cleaving swiftly through the water.

It was an eternity later when she staggered ashore and sank down beside Julio. His head was buried in his knees and he was gasping desperately for breath. She was in scarcely better shape as she stretched out on the sand.

"For Pete's sake, it's still broad daylight and you're taking a sunbath in full view of the ship."

She looked up dazedly to see Beau striding out of the waves like Poseidon. His cutoff jeans were clinging to his slim hips and strong muscular thighs and his hair was a shining bronze helmet in the sunlight. "What are you doing here?" she asked dazedly. He wasn't even breathing very hard, she thought with a touch of resentment.

"Trying to keep the two of you from being sighted by that launch," Beau said, reaching out a hand to pull her to her feet. "Come on, Julio, let's get to that cluster of trees before they decide to send out a shore party. Daniel's trying to distract them, but it would only take a glance for them to spot us."

"Right," Julio gasped, and staggered to his

feet to follow them the short distance to the grove of palm trees.

Beau's arm around her waist was strong and secure as he half led, half carried her to the shadowy shelter of the trees and she unconsciously leaned against that strength. She'd be all right in a minute, she assured herself. It wouldn't hurt to let him be the protector, the strong one for a while. She sank down and leaned against the rough bole of a palm tree and closed her eyes.

"Are you okay?"

She opened her eyes. "You shouldn't have followed us, Beau," she said wearily.

"So I was just supposed to sail away and let you take your chances?" Beau shook his head and for an instant anger flickered in his eyes. "You forgot to mention what would happen if it was the police and not Despard who captured you."

"It wouldn't have changed anything. I would still have had to come anyway," Kate said. "I had to get the Cessna."

"Without a passport the danger was increased a hundredfold." Beau dropped down across from her. "You knew that and you came anyway." She opened her lips to speak and he held up his hand. "Forget it, I've heard it all before. You owed a debt." His gaze darted to Julio sitting a few yards away. "I can see how Julio could be without a passport considering the manner of his exit from El Salvador, but why the hell don't you have one? Brenden said your mother was an American nightclub entertainer."

"I was born in Rio. When my mother left she took my birth certificate with her. Without it, Jeffrey couldn't apply for a passport for me." She shrugged. "He wasn't concerned about it at the time. In his line of work he never entered a country through the usual channels anyway. It wasn't really necessary."

"Oh no, it wasn't really necessary," Beau repeated sarcastically. "It just kept you from going to school and getting an education that might have assured your future. It stripped you of any protection you might have had from your mother's country. It's kept you lingering on the fringes of life instead of being able to participate." His lips twisted. "Hardly worth mentioning."

"I got along all right," Kate said defensively. "It's not as ugly a picture as you're painting."

"You're absolutely incredible." Beau shook his head wonderingly. "You actually believe that?"

"Of course I do," Kate said, rubbing her forehead wearily. "My life hasn't been all that bad. I've been really lucky in a number of ways." She straightened briskly. "But none of that is important right now. We've got to get started if we want to get to my place before dark."

"Your place?" Beau asked, puzzled. "You mean Brenden's cottage that you mentioned?"

She shook her head. "That's on the outskirts of Mariba. I have my own place here on this end of the island. Sometimes it was a little awkward for Jeffrey to have me around."

"I just bet it was," he muttered darkly. "So he let you come out here in the middle of the wilds on your own?"

"I wanted it that way," she said simply. "Particularly when men like Despard made it a habit of dropping by at all hours of the day and night. It was nice to have a place of my own to run away to and just be by myself." Her eyes moved back to his. "Besides, it was very near the plane.

We needed someone close by at all times to guard it."

"Oh yes, the plane," Beau drawled. "If you want to get the Cessna off the island tonight, we'd better get moving." He stood up and reached down a hand to pull her to her feet. "It's almost sunset."

She cast a glance at the fiery scarlet and delicate lavender that touched the clouds with beauty and the sea with mirrored paths of brilliance. "We still have forty minutes or so. That should give us enough time to get to my house."

He frowned. "What about the plane?"

She shook her head. "We can't leave the island now." Her blue eyes were troubled. "Not until we're sure Captain Seifert and the crew are going to be okay. You may be sure your company can get him out of this, but I can't leave until I *know*. It's my fault they were captured in the first place."

"But I told you—"

"They're my responsibility," Kate said stubbornly. "I can't leave until I know they're safe."

There was a curious tenderness mixed with the exasperation in his eyes. "Now how did I know you'd feel like that?" He ruffled her damp curls. "All right, Kate, we'll do it your way. How do we obtain this reassurance you're so set upon?"

"I can get it." Julio spoke up. "I can go to Mariba tomorrow morning with Consuello when she takes in the day's catch of fish. It shouldn't be difficult to ask a few questions at the market-place."

"Who's Consuello?"

"One of Julio's women," Kate supplied absently. "She lives in a fishing village just around the cove. Her father and brother are fishermen and so was her husband. She's a widow now."

"*One* of Julio's women?" Beau murmured. "Evidently a very advanced eighteen-year-old, Julio."

Julio grinned, his dark face shrewd. "And you were another, I'd bet. How many lovers did you have to your credit at the same age?"

"I was too much of a gentleman to count," Beau drawled. "And so should you be."

Julio shrugged. "Consuello is lonely. I merely fill a need." His eyes were suddenly twinkling. "Actually a variety of needs." He stood up. "The more I think about it, the more I believe it's my solemn duty to look up Consuello and persuade her to take me to Mariba," he said expansively. "Don't worry, Kate. I'll get on it right away."

"Or on her?" Beau suggested, his lips twitching.

Julio winked. "At any rate I'll be back by tomorrow evening at the latest with news of the captain."

"That would probably be the safest move." Kate bit her lip. "Despard's men don't know you and Consuello would be a good cover. Just be careful, Julio."

"Yes, by all means," Beau said. "Or Kate will probably be storming the local bastille to get you out."

"I'll be careful," Julio promised, touching her cheek with a gentle finger. "You, too, *pequeña.*" He turned to Beau with gruff sternness. "Watch over her." Then he was walking swiftly toward the headland using the trees as a cover.

Kate's throat felt suddenly tight and aching as she watched him swagger jauntily out of sight. "He's so young," she murmured. "What if something happens to him?"

"You told me yourself that he was older than

his years," Beau said gently. "He'll be fine, Kate." He took her hand in his, the firm vital clasp giving comfort and strength and infinite reassurance. "And if not, I'll help you storm that bastille myself."

Her smile was a little watery. "Promise?"

He nodded. "Promise. Now what will it take to get you to lead me to this house of yours?" He made a face. "I hope it has bathing facilities. I need to wash this salt water off me. I feel as if I'm going to dry up and blow away any minute."

"Oh yes, it has bathing facilities," Kate said happily, her hand unconsciously tightening on his. Such a warm strong hand, it felt so wonderfully protective and affectionate. She started off through the palm grove into the half-light of the rain forest beyond. "I'll take you there right away."

"A tree house!" Beau said blankly, his gaze taking in the upper branches of the rain tree they were standing beneath. "You've got to be kidding."

Kate shook her head. "It's really a very practical

idea," she said, her eyes wide and earnest. "The branches and foliage offer a certain amount of shelter from the sun and the rain and it's very private." She was dragging a ladder from behind a cluster of nearby bushes and he moved automatically to help her set it against the tree. "Julio and I built it. It took us about four months, but it was worth all that time."

"I can tell," he said gently. Even in the twilight dimness of the rain forest he could see the glowing eagerness in her face and it filled him with a poignant tenderness. Child-woman, vulnerability and strength. "I can't wait to look inside."

"It's not very fancy." Kate was climbing the ladder swiftly and her voice drifted down to him as he started after her. "It wasn't all that easy to furnish it. We had to use a pulley except for the little pieces we could carry." She reached the wooden platform and opened the rough wooden door with a little flourish. *"Mi casa, su casa."*

"Thank you," Beau said gravely as he preceded her into the little house.

She followed him quickly. "Perhaps you'd better let me go first. It's pretty dark in here and I know my way around." She was fumbling at the natural rattan nightstand. Suddenly a match flickered and he could see that she was lighting an old-fashioned oil lamp. She turned to face him and her eyes widened in surprise. In the cut-off jeans, bare-chested and barefooted, he was a strange wild figure in her familiar little room. Wild and virile and overpoweringly male. "It's a little close in here," she said breathlessly. "I'd better open the shutters."

"I'll do it." He was at the large square window beside the door unfastening the tan woven hemp shutters and throwing them wide. "The whole place smells of flowers." He turned and suddenly grinned. "No wonder, you have enough flora in here to fill a florist shop."

"I love flowers," she said simply. "And they grow wild in the rain forest, so I can gather fresh ones every day." She gazed around in blissful satisfaction. "They make everything look so lovely."

The simple furnishings of the room definitely needed that embellishment, she thought. There was no bed, merely a single mattress covered with blue denim on the rough-hewn floor. Other than that, there were two rattan captain's chests against two walls and the small rattan night-stand. But there were blossoms everywhere. Gorgeous coral orchids with creamy centers tumbling out of rattan holders fixed to the un-finished walls. Delicate maidenfern surrounded deep purple violets in a polished black bowl on one of the chests. A tall vase in one corner was filled to overflowing with greenery and strange white blossoms with golden markings. But his eyes were on her, not the furnishings and she was suddenly conscious of that queer breathless-ness again. "I guess it must seem primitive to you," she said uncertainly.

He shook his head slowly. "No, it's very beau-tiful and very, very special," he said quietly. "I can see how you'd be proud of it." His eyes met hers across the room and it was as if she were being wrapped in a velvet intimacy so complete it filled the whole world. "In a way it's like you. Different and lovely and totally special." He looked away and his eyes fell on a colorful ob-ject on the rattan chest across the room. "What's that?"

She was glad he'd been distracted. She didn't know if she could have broken the intimate moment herself. She followed his gaze with her own and then smiled eagerly. "That's my music box." She ran across the room and knelt by the chest. Her hands lifted the scarlet-and-ivory carousel with loving care and wound the key at the bottom. "I discovered it in a pawn shop in Port of Spain. Isn't it lovely? A carousel with not only horses but unicorns and centaurs. It was in pretty bad shape when I bought it, but I re-painted it and Julio found a man to fix the mech-anism." She set the music box back on the chest and stayed there, her eyes misty with dreams as she watched the carousel turn slowly on its pedestal. "I've always loved the tune it plays. I tried to find out what it was, but the man in the shop didn't know and neither did Julio and Jeffrey."

"It's 'Lara's Theme' from *Dr. Zhivago*," Beau said, his voice husky.

"*Dr. Zhivago?*"

"A beautiful movie taken from a book by Pasternak. I have a copy of the book in my cabin on the *Searcher*. I'll give it to you once we're back on board."

"Thank you. I'd like that." Her gaze was still

fixed dreamily on the carousel. "You know, I've always wanted to ride a carousel. I was at a carnival in a little village in Nicaragua once, but it didn't have a merry-go-round."

"I'll buy you one."

"What?" She turned to look at him in bewilderment.

"I'll buy you the best damn carousel in the whole world," he said thickly. "Hell, I'll buy you an entire amusement park." He wanted to give her everything she'd never had. The experience, the beauty, the knowledge. He *needed* to give them to her.

She laughed uncertainly. "You're joking." She rose to her feet. "For a moment I thought you were serious."

He opened his lips to speak but quickly closed them again. "We'll talk about it later," he said. "Now where can I get rid of this combination of salt and sweat that's coating me? You promised me a bath." He looked around with a whimsical smile. "Somehow I don't think your very special house has a bathroom."

"There's a spring-fed pool several yards north of here," she said with a grin. She picked up the carousel and set it carefully on the floor before opening the chest. "It's a little cold, but very clear."

"That's where you sunbathe?"

There was something in the smoky darkness of his eyes that caused a frisson of heat to tingle through her. "Yes, that's the place," she said, quickly reaching into the chest to pull out soap, a large folded terry towel, and shampoo. "It won't be very warm there now. It's almost dark."

"You only have one towel."

Her eyes flew to meet his and what she saw there made the heat in her loins turn molten.

"We'll need at least two," he said with slow deliberation. "You're all salty too." His voice dropped to velvet softness. "But don't worry, I'll wash every grain of it off you personally." He smiled intimately. "Very personally."

She drew a deep breath. "You want me to go with you?"

"I insist upon it," he murmured. "I always did have a lousy sense of direction. I might get lost in the forest and never be heard from again."

"Then I guess I'd better come along," she said,

reaching for a few more towels and a white cotton caftan. "I may need to redeem that promise you made to help me storm the bastille." Her voice was as light as his, and didn't reflect the fact that her heart was pounding so hard she felt as if she'd been running.

She didn't dare keep up the badinage as they made their way down the ladder and along the path to the pool. She wasn't experienced enough to maintain that casual sophistication and was sure that at any moment she'd betray how nervous and uncertain she felt. Nervous and something else. Something exciting and moving and as beautifully primitive as the rain forest surrounding them.

It was almost pitch-dark as they reached the bank of the pool, and the water was only discernible from the bank by the occasional glitter of moonlight on its mirror surface.

Kate dropped her towels and the caftan on the bank. "It's shallow enough to stand upright around the edges. It only deepens as you go toward the middle."

"Right." Beau had already stripped off his meager clothes and was jumping into the water.

"Damn!" he exploded. "Where does that spring originate, the South Pole?"

She burst out laughing. "I told you it was cold."

"*Cold,* not frigid. Throw me the soap, will you?"

She tossed it to him and then pulled the T-shirt over her head. There was no use being shy. Beau had seen everything there was to see last night on the *Searcher.* Besides, it was so dark here Beau was hardly more than a bronze blur though only a few feet away. It was reasonable to assume she'd be equally indiscernible.

She inhaled sharply as she jumped into the water and she heard Beau's chuckle. "Definitely the South Pole, eh?"

"Definitely," she gasped. She poured a little shampoo in her hand and began rubbing it into her hair. The curls were coarse and wiry with salt and she sudsed and rinsed it twice before she was satisfied it was clean. "I've finished with the shampoo. Would you like to use it?"

"I made do with the soap," he said carelessly. His voice was suddenly much closer and she looked up to see him only a few feet away. "I didn't want to wait. I wanted to get through in a hurry so I could have my treat."

"Your treat?" She moistened her lips nervously.

"Bathing Kate, bonny Kate, the prettiest Kate in Christendom."

"Shakespeare," she identified, a trifle breathlessly.

"Right," he drawled, "but we're not going to discuss literature tonight. That I promise you, sweet Kate. I only display that degree of restraint every century or so."

"I think most of the salt is washed off now," she offered faintly.

"But we have to be sure, don't we? I promised you *every* grain of salt." He was very close now and she could see the white flash of his teeth in his darkly shadowed face. "And I'll think we'll start here."

The cold wet bar was against her throat and she gave an involuntary shiver. "Cold?" he murmured. "Let's see if we can fix that." He rubbed the soap briskly between his hands. "I'm going to like this much better anyway. And you will too, Kate. I guarantee that you'll like it a hell of a lot better."

He took the bottle of shampoo from her and tossed it and the soap on the bank. Then his hands were on her throat rubbing the lather from his hands into her skin with slow teasing skill. She stood perfectly still, almost forgetting to breathe as his hands moved to her bare shoulders rising out of the water. His hands were cold from the water and hard with calluses. Playboys shouldn't have calluses, she thought inconsequentially, but then Beau wasn't a stereotype. He was a law unto himself. His hands weren't really cold either. She could feel the vital heat beneath the surface coolness and it was arousing an answering heat everywhere he touched.

"Give me your left arm."

She raised her arm from the water and his hands moved over it from shoulder to wrist with slow easy strokes that should have been soothing. They weren't. By the time he'd finished the other arm, her heart was beating wildly and her flesh was so exquisitely sensitive that every brush of his hands was actually painful. It was like something from an erotic fantasy to be standing here in this icy water in almost total darkness while a naked shadowy stranger ran his hands over her body in this intimately arousing fashion. Yet Beau wasn't really a stranger. They'd been through so much together that in some ways she felt she knew him far better than she did Jeffrey or Julio.

"And now the pièce de résistance," Beau drawled. His hands closed upon her breasts beneath the water. She cried out and involuntarily surged toward him.

"I've been wanting to do that since the minute I saw you in that bar," he said thickly. He was squeezing her gently and his thumbs were exploring the pink rims that encircled the hard crests of her nipples. "And I think you've been wanting it, too, haven't you, Kate?"

She hadn't realized it, but she must have. The response was so immediate, the filling of an aching void so evident. "The water has washed all the soap off your hands," she said vaguely through the haze of heat surrounding her. It seemed impossible now that she'd even noticed the coldness of the water.

"It doesn't matter, we'll never miss it," Beau

assured her. "They say friction does just as good a job as soap."

"Who says?" she asked breathlessly, not really caring. The nail of his thumb was toying playfully with the swollen tip of her breast.

"I forget," Beau said absently, moving closer, "but I'm anxious to test the theory. Part your legs, love."

She obeyed without thinking. "Why do—" She broke off as his knee suddenly was inserted between her thighs and he was lifting her, one hand moving from her breast to the curve of her buttocks to pull her forward so she was straddling his strong muscular thigh with shocking intimacy. He pressed her back against the bank, resting his other knee against it for support.

"There, that's better." Beau's voice held the same breathlessness she was feeling. "Almost comfortable." His hand at her bottom was moving her back and forth on his leg. "A very comfortable ride, eh, sugar?"

Comfortable? There was a distinctly mischievous note in that Southern drawl that made her aware he knew just how ridiculous that adjective was. That friction he'd mentioned was burning her with every motion and she felt she was learning by Braille the physical substance and textures of him. The hard bone beneath the resilient muscles, the slightly rough film of hair that was prickling against that most sensitive part of her. Her swollen breasts swung heavy and ripe against the sleek smoothness of his chest with every other movement and she could hear his breathing become harsher and more labored with every touch.

His hand still cupping her breast was squeezing and relaxing in rhythm with the molten friction he was stirring in her lower body. His index finger encircling the budding tip was both inquisitive and arousing. "You have lovely little puckers all around this pretty thing," he said raggedly. "Is that because of the cold or what I'm doing to you?"

"I don't know," she gasped. She didn't know anything that wasn't connected with the liquid aching need that was racking her entire body.

"Then perhaps we'd better find out." The hand that was on her buttocks suddenly moved around and slid swiftly between her and his thigh. "I want you to be sure. It's a matter of personal pride." His fingers started moving, caressing, delving, teasing with a devilish skill.

"Beau!" She arched forward against him, her hands clutching desperately at his shoulders. She uttered a low sound that was half guttural groan and half whimper as she felt two of those diabolically knowledgeable fingers enter, stroke, burn, rotate.

She was so close she could feel the thunder of his heart against her ear and his voice was shaking a little. "It's me, isn't it, Kate? Say it!"

"It's you," she said, hardly knowing what she was saying. She would have said anything he wanted her to at that moment.

"So tight," he muttered. "Oh, God, Kate, I can't wait. I want to be *there*."

"What?" He'd added another finger with some difficulty and she was only conscious of the sensation of fullness that pervaded her.

"I want to ride, too, Kate." He laughed a little shakily. "With your permission, milady."

She found herself trying to push down harder. "Yes, oh yes." She closed her eyes. "Whatever you like."

"What a fantastically generous invitation. I

just may take you up on it. It's going to be a long night." He pinched her nipple gently with his thumb and forefinger, sending a jolt of electricity shooting through her. "But unfortunately I don't want to start here. Maybe tomorrow I'll be ready for aquatics but tonight I want to feel all your silk and heat against me." His hand left her breast and wandered down to her waist. Then his fingers plunged forcefully upward and she gave a low gasp of pleasure. "Remember that," he said hoarsely. "Remember the feel of me. You're mine there now and I'll be back." His hand reluctantly left her and also moved to her waist. He lifted her off his thigh and up onto the bank with easy strength.

She sat there dazed and bewildered. The warm humid air felt almost chilly on her wet nude body, but it wasn't the astringent shock it should have been. For Beau was suddenly beside her on the bank picking up a towel and drying her with careful thoroughness, his hands caressing and squeezing her occasionally through the soft material.

"Bend over. I want to do your hair."

He was thorough with that also and when he

was done he combed his fingers through the damp curls before fluffing them lightly. "It's almost dry already," he commented.

"It's so short it dries very fast," she said mundanely. However, there was nothing mundane about the way she was feeling only inches away from him. She could smell the scent of soap and musk and feel the heat of his body reaching out to her.

He handed her the simple white cotton caftan. "You'd better put this on." He picked up another towel and started to dry himself.

She slipped the caftan over her head and pulled it down over her body. Even the loose folds of material were a teasing provocation against her flesh that Beau had sensitized so expertly. She could barely stand the touch of it against the swelling fullness of her breasts. "You haven't anything to put on."

"The only thing I want against me tonight is you," he said as he gathered the towels, shampoo, and soap. "Grab our clothes, will you? I want to get back to your place with the speed of light."

So did she and her movements were just as

swift as his. It was only a matter of moments before they were climbing the ladder to the tree house. Beau dropped the bundle he was carrying on the wooden platform but stopped her as she would have opened the door. "Wait," he said, drawing a deep shaky breath, "I want to hold you a moment before we go inside." He took the clothes out of her arms and dropped them carelessly on top of the pile of towels. "Just hold you. I don't think I'm going to be able to do that once we get inside. I'm hurting too much."

He took her into his arms and held her with loving gentleness. She could feel the hard urgency of his need against her, but there was only affection and tenderness in the strong clasp of his arms and the brush of his lips at her temple. He rocked her and for a moment she forgot about desire as she was drowned in that warm glowing gentleness. Beau. Oh, dear, sweet, wild Beau. She felt her heart swell with emotion as her arms went around him to hug him fiercely to her.

"Hey!" he chuckled. "Take it easy. Your enthusiasm is much appreciated but very arousing." He reached behind her to swing open the door. "We'll continue this later." He pushed her gently into the room. "Much later."

"All right." She watched him dreamily as he followed her into the room. In the glow of the oil lamp he was all sleek muscular power and dominant aroused male. Very aroused.

"Take off the gown, Kate." His eyes were dark and smoky but the golden glints were leaping.

She pulled the caftan slowly over her head but when she dropped it to the floor she realized he was no longer looking at her but across the room. There was a frown on his face and she watched him with puzzled eyes as he crossed the room to the chest against the wall.

He picked up the carousel music box she'd set on the floor when she was riffling through the rattan chest for towels and placed it with great care on the exact center of the chest. "You should be more careful," he said gruffly. "One of us might have kicked it or knocked it over. Treasures have to be taken care of."

She felt a warm glow start somewhere near her heart. "Do they?"

He nodded, his eyes grave. "Yes."

"I suppose you should know." She laughed

shakily. "A rich man like you must have quite a few of them."

"Not really. I guess you could say I have a good many valuables but that's something else again. You've got to care for something to make it a treasure." He was coming toward her with that smooth, lithe coordination. "Perhaps I didn't deserve to have a treasure before. Maybe I would have been too careless and irresponsible to care for it properly." He stopped before her and his lopsided smile was boyishly endearing. "I wouldn't be that careless now, Kate. Will you be my treasure if I promise to guard and cherish you very carefully?"

The words were so simply eloquent, his expression so beautiful that she couldn't speak for an instant because of the lump in her throat. His treasure for an eternity or merely for tonight? Somehow at this moment it didn't make any difference. One night with Beau would be worth any pain she would have to suffer later.

"If that's what you want me to be," she said breathlessly.

"That's what I want." His hand reached up to cup the curve of her cheek with infinite gentleness. "You won't regret it, Kate." A dark frown suddenly clouded his face. "This doesn't have anything to do with that blasted bargain we made, does it? You know that's down the drain. You really want me, right?"

"I really want you," she said, a tender smile tugging at her lips. How could he doubt it when he could see the response he'd so easily ignited in her? He seemed to ignite all kinds of responses with no effort at all—and not only the physical. Tenderness, laughter, respect, admiration, love. Love? The word had come so easily to mind that it frightened her a little. She must be very careful not to think of that. It was far too dangerous in a relationship that might prove as ephemeral as theirs.

"Then that's what you're going to get," he drawled, the lightness back in his expression. "Every bit of me that you can take." He reached out and lightly cupped her breast in his palm. "Now."

Then his arm was about her waist and he was leading her to the denim-covered mattress across the room. His fingers splayed out and rubbed her hip in a caress that was more affectionate than sensual. "I can't get enough of touching you. That incredibly silky skin with all that warm aliveness beneath it. I'm constantly wanting to reach out to play or rub against you like a cat with a satin pillow." His hands on her shoulders were pushing her to her knees on the mattress before kneeling to face her. His eyes were glazed as he stared down at her naked breasts with an intentness that caused a shiver of anticipation. "I want to do that now but I'm afraid the time for play is over."

"The light?" she asked. Perhaps she wouldn't feel so shy if she couldn't see the smoldering sensuality on his face.

He shook his head. "I like you bathed in lamplight. It gleams and shimmers on you like liquid gold." He slowly bent his head until his lips were only a breath away from one taut eager nipple. That warm breath kissed her even before his lips touched her. "Now let's see if I can make that pretty breast pucker again for me."

She inhaled sharply as his mouth closed around her as he began to alternately nibble and suckle at the nipple that had been waiting eagerly for his attention. He was very gentle at first but she could feel the change in him as the moments passed. There was a tension and restrained savagery in the way he pushed her on her back on the mattress. Both hands were encircling her breast, now causing it to swell into prominence. His mouth seemed to be trying to envelop the entire mound at times while his tongue flicked wildly over every portion of it. His nips became sharper and his face was flushed and heavy above her. "I can't get enough of you. I want to eat you alive." He suckled strongly and she arched up to him with a little cry. He was over her now, his lips still working frantically at her breast. He began rubbing against her like the cat he'd compared himself to and it was as erotic as his lips at her breast. Yet there was nothing of the sleek feline about Beau in that moment. He was all hard bone and supple muscles and aroused male.

She could feel that arousal brush against her as he moved and she unconsciously opened her thighs to welcome him. She wanted to welcome all of him, touch, smell, sight. She wanted him to surround her in every way possible.

"You want me?" he asked, his eyes blazing

almost pure gold. His hand traveled down to rest possessively between her thighs, not moving or caressing. However, just the warm heaviness of it against that most private part of her so vulnerably open to him filled her with unbearable excitement. His voice was harsh with restraint. "Here? Now? You're ready for me?"

"I want you." It was a gasp. *"Now!"*

He closed his eyes and breathed a shuddering sigh of relief. "Thank heaven, I didn't know how long I could keep up this foreplay. I'm nearly wild." He was parting her thighs with frantic eagerness, his fingers now moving, caressing, exploring. "You're so pretty here." He lowered his head to her belly, gently nipping the soft rounded flesh. "And you *are* ready for me." He laughed huskily. "I wanted to make sure. You're so beautifully tight I was afraid I'd hurt you if you weren't as wild for me as I am for you."

He didn't have to worry about that, she thought hazily. She was aching frantically with a feverish desire for completion.

He was between her thighs, his hard warmth nudging against her and he suddenly smiled down at her with loving sweetness. "I'll be careful," he whispered. "There's no way I'd ever want to hurt you. I told you I know how to care for treasures now."

Poignant tenderness and passion were in his voice and his eyes. . . . They were so beautiful she felt tears rise in her own. Everything was beautiful, his golden eyes, the sensual curve of his lips, the brilliant coral orchids on the wall beyond his shoulder, but most of all the feel of him as he became part of her.

"Relax." There was a touch of impatience in his voice. "I told you I wouldn't hurt you. Don't you trust me?"

Of course she trusted him, but there was something the matter. There was a hint of troubled hurt in his face and she couldn't bear it. Nothing must spoil the beauty of what was happening to both of them, she thought dreamily. Not when she could take care of the problem so easily.

She surged upward with determined forcefulness and there was a sharp piercing pain that was immediately drowned in the equally sharp delight of being full of him. She smiled happily up at him. "Better?"

"Better," he echoed blankly, his face stunned.

He flexed spasmodically and a great shudder racked him. He closed his eyes. "Oh, Lord, yes, that's better."

"Good." Her hands caressed his hips lovingly. "I want you to be happy, Beau."

His lids lifted and he looked down at her with a curious expression of torment. "I know you do," he said hoarsely. "Everyone has to be happy even if it means the giving has to go on forever. Because we all keep taking, don't we?" His lips twisted bitterly. "Even me. For once in my life I wanted to give, but I'm taking too." One hand reached up to gently stroke her cheek. "And the damnable part of it is that I can't stop now."

She was bewildered. She'd wanted to help him, but he looked so sad now. "Beau, should I—"

"Shhh." His fingers were on her lips. "Hush, everything's all right. I'm going to take, but I'll find a way of giving too. Maybe it will all even out." He was moving with a slow stroking thrust, letting her get used to him. It wasn't easy for him to maintain that control. She was conscious of the leashed urgency in him struggling to break the bonds of restraint. She could feel the knotted muscles of his hips beneath her palms. The stroking was hotly tantalizing but still she wanted more. She wanted that primitive animal passion he'd shown her before. She *needed* it.

"Beau." Her murmur was feverish as her nails dug unconsciously into the flesh of his hips. She surged against him urgently. "Please, Beau."

She could see the conflict on his face and then he gave a helpless groan. "Kate. Oh, *damn*, Kate." And thrust forward forcefully, taking her breath, burning, pressing, thrusting until she was almost mindless with pleasure.

Treasure. A carousel playing a haunting melody, Beau's golden eyes, his hand in hers walking through the rain forest, a mocking Southern drawl with a note of underlying tenderness, courage, honesty, passion, this beautiful, throbbing rhythm. So many treasures. He was giving them all to her and when he gave the final radiant gift that made rapture seem commonplace, it was no more precious than the other treasures he'd heaped upon her.

Her head was cradled in the hollow of his shoulder and she could feel the hard thud of his heart beneath her ear. Its cadence was gradually lessening, as was her own. His hand automatically tangled in her curls and began to thread through them with lazy contentment. "So silky," he murmured. "Did I tell you how much I loved those soft little ringlets?"

She nodded. "You're certainly a very tactile person, Beau," she charged teasingly, then suddenly chuckled. "Not that I'd be so ungrateful as to complain in the present set of circumstances."

She could feel him stiffen against her and his hand paused in her hair. "No, you wouldn't complain no matter what I did to you," he said quietly. "You wouldn't care to tell me how you happen to be a virgin? I received the distinct impression from the lady I was with in Alvarez's bar that you were every bit as experienced as she."

"Did you?" she asked, blissfully uncaring. "I was in there quite often prying Jeffrey away from the whiskey bottle. She probably misunderstood." Her head lifted suddenly as she gazed at him in troubled uncertainty. "Does it bother you?"

"You're damn right it bothers me. I'm not

accustomed to deflowering virgins. Why the devil didn't you tell me?" His lips twisted. "Lord, I was even telling you what a meager price I was exacting for my services."

"It was cheap," she said quietly. "Getting Jeffrey away from Castellano was important to me. In comparison the other didn't matter at all."

"It was important enough to keep you a virgin until now."

"The men I've come across seem to look upon women as something to be used." Her tone became fierce. "I won't be used! I have worth."

"Yes, you have worth." He touched her cheek with gossamer gentleness. "It can't have been very easy for you considering the life you've led."

She shrugged. "I can take care of myself. It's been easier lately with Julio around."

"And before Julio was around?"

"I just told anyone who bothered me that I had VD," she said simply. "Jeffrey said it would work and most of the time it did. Men seem to be very frightened when you mention that."

He chuckled. "It's a wonder you ever got away with it if you looked at them the way you're looking at me." Her eyes were as clear and solemn as a little girl's. "I don't think you've ever learned to lie very well."

"You're right. I hate it." She suddenly shivered. "But it's much easier when you're frightened."

He felt a sudden fierce anger at the thought of Kate alone and afraid. It was so intense it caught him off guard. He couldn't remember ever before experiencing that sense of outrage. He had to draw a deep breath and consciously force his tense muscles to relax. "They must have been very fainthearted types," he said gruffly. "I guarantee I wouldn't have been so easy to get rid of even if I'd believed you."

Her eyes widened. "You wouldn't?"

He grasped her by the shoulders and tumbled her back into his arms. "Nope. Not with a very special lady like you." He brushed a butterfly kiss on the tip of her nose. "First, I'd have sent you to the best doctor available to start your cure. Then I'd have whisked you away and spent your entire convalescent period showing you how many wonderful ways we could pleasure each other with no danger at all to either of us."

"What ways?" Her eyes were bright with curiosity.

"I'll demonstrate later. It loses something in the telling."

"Well, I don't see how it could have been any better than what we've just had." She raised her head to gaze at him mistily. "It was so beautiful."

"Was it, Kate?" His voice was husky. She was so dear, like a happy little girl. "I'm glad it was like that for you."

"Oh, it was." Her blue eyes were full of dreams. "You made it that way, Beau. I wish I could give you something just as valuable." She brushed her lips lovingly over the pulse beat in the hollow of his throat. "I'd like to give you rare spices, precious stones, and one hundred twenty talents of gold."

"One hundred twenty talents?" Beau asked, puzzled.

She nodded. "That's what the Queen of Sheba brought as gifts to Solomon."

The creases in the corners of his eyes deepened as he laughed up at her. "I should have known." He shook his head ruefully. "That brain of yours is filled with the most amazing trivia." He kissed her quickly to banish the troubled frown that was beginning to form. "Fascinating trivia from a fascinating lady. And for your information, my services are not to be bought with one hundred twenty talents of gold. They're considered absolutely priceless in some circles. So you may keep your gifts, Kate."

"Really?" Her eyes were suddenly dancing with mischief. "I bet I know one gift you'll accept." She pulled away from him and jumped to her feet. "You, being such a very tactile gentleman." Ignoring his growl of protest, she picked up the white caftan and pulled it over her head. She ran to the far corner of the room and began turning a crank high up on the wall. "This took an entire week for Julio and me to set up, but I think it was worth it. It's rigged with a pulley outside."

She heard an exclamation of surprise behind her and looked up at the ceiling that was rolling neatly back to reveal leafy branches and moonlit sky. "I wanted to lie under the stars." She glanced over her shoulder and made a face. "Unfortunately, I can't do this very often. Birds seem to find my flowers too attractive. I woke up one morning and found a parrot trying to build a nest in my orchids." The roof was completely rolled back now and she released the crank and strolled back to him. "I thought it was very inconsiderate of her since she had millions of other orchids in the forest to choose from." She dropped to her knees beside him. "I don't see why she had to . . ." She trailed off. "Why are you looking at me so strangely?"

"Was I?" he asked absently. The lamplight was touching her sun-streaked curls with an aureole of radiance. The same radiance that was in her eyes. He pulled her down into his arms cradling her and pressing her head once more into the hollow of his shoulder. "I didn't realize I was doing it. Perhaps I'm not used to women who live in tree houses with roofs that roll back so they can see the stars."

"Well, then they've missed something really special," she said staunchly, nestling closer. "Look at that night sky. It seems close enough so you can reach out and touch it." She chuckled. "That should appeal to you. Midnight blue velvet for you to stroke. Do you like your gift, Beau?"

"Oh yes, I like my gift." The soft warm breeze stirred the branches above them and the scent of rich earth, wildflowers, and wet grass was all around them now. The sky was midnight blue velvet and the stars were as clear and beautiful as Kate's eyes. His hand began to stroke her curls once again as he fought against the most unmanly lump that persisted in forming in his throat. "My lovely, silken Kate and a blue velvet sky. How could I help but like it?"

Six

THE FIRST GRAY light of dawn was filtering through the glossy green of the leaves above her and she shivered unconsciously and drew closer to Beau's comforting warmth. And he *was* warm, she thought drowsily, warm and hard and yet . . .

She opened her eyes to see his face only inches from her own and felt a queer tugging at her heart. He looked so vulnerable with all the cynicism and mockery banished by sleep. His long lashes were tipped with gold at the ends. She hadn't realized that, and his bronze hair had those same golden streaks woven through its darkness. He was so beautiful. She reached up with a careful finger to touch one of those lashes casting shadows on the hard plane of his cheek. The lash fluttered and she jerked her finger away quickly. She didn't want to wake him. When he was awake he would assume once more all the armor he used to guard himself from the world. When he was asleep, she could pretend that he belonged to her; awake such fantasizing about him was hard to sustain. The sadness of the thought served to jolt her out of her lovely dreamy euphoria.

Of course, he didn't belong to her. A night of passion meant nothing to a man. She should know that by now. Julio and Jeffrey had been prime examples of that philosophy and the other men she'd been exposed to over the years had been just the same. However special last night had been to her, she mustn't expect the same response from Beau. They were almost strangers and he might be equally tender and loving to any woman who'd given him sexual pleasure. How did she know? How did she know anything about the way he thought or felt?

She began to edge away, careful not to wake him. She felt a sudden desire to put up a few defenses of her own. She was the vulnerable one, not Beau. Not only by the nature of their bargain, but by her love for him. Last night, try as she might, she'd been unable to keep that knowledge at bay. She loved him and for her that emotion was synonymous with commitment. A commitment with Beau was very dangerous but she had no choice now. She only knew one way to love and the affection she felt for Jeffrey and Julio seemed minute in comparison.

With the utmost care she slid off the mattress and stood up. She gathered a few towels from the chest and snatched her white caftan from the floor beside the mattress. Then she let herself quietly out the door.

Thirty minutes later she'd bathed in the pool and was stretched out on her towel on the mossy bank basking in the early morning sunshine. Even this early the tropical rays were direct and hot on her naked flesh but she wasn't tempted to take shelter under the overhanging trees or in the cold clear pool. It was pure sensual bliss to feel that marvelous heat soaking into her bones. She'd always loved the sun. How did people exist in frigid climates where ice and snow were the norm?

Ice. Beau had spent years on the ice as a vocation.

Strange to think of that. Beau seemed to be meant for the sun just as she was. Golden eyes, golden skin, and that easy golden charm. Well, maybe not so easy, she thought drowsily, there had been moments when he'd displayed a complexity and harshness that had surprised and bewildered her. In fact, those moments had been quite frequent in their short acquaintance. It was just difficult to remember them when his half-tender, half-savage lovemaking was still so fresh in her memory. A golden memory too. . . .

The deft hands parting her thighs were strong and gentle and very familiar. Beau. A happy smile curved her lips, though she didn't bother to open her eyes. It seemed far too much trouble and it was so pleasant just lying here, letting the powerful sun pour down upon her and Beau flow into her with one slow easy stroke. Once joined he seemed content and was still. She could feel his hands slowly stroking her curls before moving down to caress with gossamer gentleness her shoulders and breasts and the soft flesh of her belly. The sun was hot upon her, his hands gently caressing her and his manhood both hotly passionate and warmly affectionate within her.

She'd never imagined the two could exist side by side and she opened her eyes to tell him so.

His face was heavy and intent above her and his lips beautifully sensual as he began to flex slowly, almost lazily, within her.

"Beau."

"Shhh," he said huskily. "Don't speak. You look like a lovely sacrifice to Ra in the sunlight. I couldn't resist coming into you and accepting in his place. Just relax and let me play. We have all the time in the world and I love to feel the heat of you around me."

His hands were drifting lightly over her, touching, caressing, and touching again. Not demanding, just grasping and then releasing much as he might delicately stroke the feathers of a bird before releasing it to let it fly away. His rhythm within her had the same delicacy and possessiveness and her lashes drifted shut once more.

"That's right, Kate." Beau's murmur was velvet soft. "I told you I wanted to flow over you like golden rain. Just let me warm and fulfill you." His fingers were between her thighs skillfully searching and caressing and suddenly she inhaled sharply, her lashes flying open.

"Like that?" Beau smiled lazily down at her. "I thought you would. I love to hear you gasp and look at me all wide-eyed like a little girl who's just been given a present." He suddenly thrust forward, touching, teasing, filling, and she was abruptly no longer even a little bit drowsy.

"I'm sorry to disappoint you but you're not warming me now, Beau." Her voice was a trifle breathless. "You're burning."

"That's the risk you run when you lie naked in the sun," he said thickly, his hands sliding around to cup her buttocks so as to bring himself deeper into that heat that was now turning molten for both of them. "But I'll try to make this particular burn as pleasurable as possible."

She found he was a man of his word. Burn her he did, but it was with a flame so exquisite it would have been pure agony to quench it. It was strangely unreal to be lying here in this little circle of brilliant sunlight in the lush dusky greenness of the rain forest. It was as if the two of them were enveloped in a spotlight that was ambivalently both starkly revealing and blurred to a dreamlike haze.

Heat without, heat within. Silence except for

the sound of Beau's harsh uneven breathing and her own occasional gasp and murmur of satisfaction and delight, the scent of soap, musk, and the earth beneath them. Heat without, burning within. Beau's golden eyes narrowed intently on her face, his hips moving with smooth explosive power, the patches of sky through the trees, not midnight but sapphire velvet now. Burning without, burning within. Beau's hands lifting, her own cry, almost a sob, the deepening, the power, the burning. Oh, dear heaven, the sweet heady burning! Within, without, surrounding, consuming. The burning!

Beau was collapsed upon her, his chest laboring as if he were starved for oxygen. His hands on her hips were still sealing her to him as if unwilling to relinquish possession as he had passion. She found her hands on his shoulders grasping him with that same desperation. Not yet. Let it go on. Beauty always faded so swiftly. Just this time, let it go on.

"I'm too heavy for you." He was shifting and rolling off her, his breathing coming in gasps. "Lord, I'm sorry, Kate. I must have nearly crushed you."

"If you did, I didn't notice," Kate said lightly. She nestled closer, her fingers curling in the springy thatch of hair on his chest. Her lashes demurely veiled the sudden mischief in her eyes. "But then, I was otherwise occupied."

He chuckled. "But not productively, I trust." His grin gradually faded. That unthinking remark had struck too close to home to be considered amusing. He'd been indulging in light sophisticated badinage as if she were just any woman. But she wasn't just any woman, this was Kate and must be protected and cared for. A task he hadn't been doing with any degree of success lately, he thought grimly. He sat up and then slipped from the bank into the icy water. "I think I feel the need for a cold swim," he said tersely. "It would have probably been a better idea if I'd taken it first." He struck out with brisk strokes toward the center of the pool.

Kate sat up, gazing after him in bewilderment. It was clear that Beau was upset, but the change from laughter to grimness had been so abrupt that it was difficult to comprehend. What had upset him so much? Then she experienced an icy chill that was worse than Beau had felt when he'd slipped into the pool. Pregnancy. Beau was afraid she might become pregnant and hold him responsible. It was the only explanation for his sudden withdrawal and then almost harsh rejection.

She slipped off the bank, scarcely noticing the coldness of the water on her sun-warmed skin. She hadn't even considered the consequences of their lovemaking before, but it wouldn't have upset her unduly if she had. Illegitimacy didn't necessarily mean being unloved as she had been. If she did become pregnant she would be sure her child was nurtured and surrounded by love. She mustn't feel hurt at Beau's reaction to the idea of her having his child. Perhaps he didn't know her well enough to realize that she wouldn't expect any support or help from him if that came to pass. Still, the soul-chilling depression remained and she suddenly didn't want to face Beau until the memory of that curt rejection faded a little.

She levered herself onto the bank and dried off briskly and put on the white caftan. She didn't look back as she walked swiftly down the path toward the tree house.

She was already dressed in her customary blue

jeans and was buttoning up a soft white cotton shirt when Beau strode through the door. He'd slipped on his cutoff blue jeans that were still wet and obviously freshly laundered. He was frowning moodily as he shut the door. "Why the hell didn't you tell me you were leaving? I looked away for a minute and when I looked back you were gone."

"I didn't see any reason in staying around," she said quietly, rolling up the long sleeves of the shirt to elbow length. "It was time I got dressed anyway and there wasn't any need to disturb you." She ran her fingers carelessly through her damp curls. "I won't be gone long. I'm afraid there's nothing much to do here. All my books are in the other chest if you'd like to glance through them. If you're hungry, there's a tin of canned ham and some bottled orange juice in there as well."

"Gone," he echoed blankly, his eyes darkening stormily. "And may I ask where you think you're going without me?"

"I have to go check the plane. There's no use both of us going. The glade is only a short distance from here and I should be back in less than an hour."

The cool logic of her argument appeared not to faze him at all. "*We* should be back in an hour," he said grimly. "I thought I made it clear that we were a team now."

She avoided his eyes as she thrust her feet into tennis shoes and then knelt to tie them. "There's nothing really clear between us, is there? And you certainly shouldn't feel any responsibility for me." She stood up and her eyes met his steadily. "I can take care of myself. I have for a number of years and there's no reason for me to stop now." She paused meaningfully. "No reason at all." Her eyes widened in surprise as he muttered a curse. Now what was he upset about? She'd thought he'd be relieved to know she wouldn't be a problem to him. Perhaps he still didn't understand. "We had a bargain. Whatever happens I'll accept it as part of it."

"For God's sake, shut up!" he bit out. "That idiotic bargain has nothing to do with us. Not anymore. What kind of man do you think I am? The woman I made that bargain with never really existed. You've been a damn victim all your life and if you think I'm going to continue the trend you're out of your mind." He ran his fingers distractedly through his hair and a sun-streaked lock fell carelessly over his forehead. "And now you're hinting that if you were to have my child, I should just turn and walk away and forget you. Quite the little martyr. Too bad your rain forest doesn't have a lion or two I could throw you to."

"There's no reason for you to get so upset. I just wanted you to know how I felt."

"I'm damn well aware how you feel. You're so used to coming last and letting everyone impose on you that you expect me to do the same." His lips tightened. "Well, I'm not about to satisfy any masochistic tendencies you might be harboring. I'm going to take care of you whether you like it or not." He drew a deep breath. "I know it may be too late to prevent you from becoming pregnant, but I'll do my damnedest to keep my hands off you from now on."

She felt a pain so fierce it made her a little ill. "That's not necessary," she said numbly. "We made a bar—"

"Screw the bargain," he said roughly. "Will you listen to me? There isn't any bargain and last night and this morning didn't exist. When I get you off this island, I'm going to take you back to the States and establish you in Connecticut with two friends of mine. Dany and Anthony will take good care of you." He frowned thoughtfully. "I'll hire a tutor for you until you're ready to enter college and then we'll choose one close enough so that you can come home weekends. You'll like Briarcliff and Dany will make you very welcome."

"Dany?" Kate asked bewilderedly.

"Dany Malik, an old friend. I coached her for six years before she won the gold medal for figure skating at the Calgary Olympics two years ago."

"That's the old friend you mentioned being in bondage to," Kate said slowly, feeling a twinge of jealousy. "You must have cared for her very much."

"She and Anthony are my best friends," he said simply. "And they'll take excellent care of you. Dany and Anthony are on tour with the ice show only a few months out of every year and the rest of the time they stay at Briarcliff. It's just the kind of stable lifestyle that you need."

"Wait a minute." She held up her hand. "I can't take all this in. Where are you going to be in this grand scheme of things?"

"I'll be around," he said evasively. "At least until we make sure you're—"

"Not pregnant," she supplied crisply. "How very kind of you." She folded her arms across her chest to still their trembling. "I suppose I should be grateful for your generosity. I hope you'll forgive me if I'm not. I don't need either your kindness or your generosity. I don't need anything from you." She crossed the room and tried to pass by him on her way to the door. "Now that we understand each other I'd like to—"

He grabbed her by the shoulders and shook her. "We *don't* understand each other and you're not leaving here until we do. I've seen too much of that kind of insanity in relationships to let it happen to me." His eyes were blazing into hers. "Okay, I'm not going to stick around once I set you up at Briarcliff. Do you have any idea of how much I want you? I want to touch, fondle, enter—and not necessarily in that order, as I proved down at the pool. I told you I wasn't a boy, but I've been acting like one. How long do you think I'd be able to restrain myself from dragging you to the nearest motel every weekend if I stayed within reaching distance?" He dragged her closer and jutted his hips forward so that she could feel his bold arousal. "For Pete's sake, look at me now! I've just told you I wouldn't touch you and it wouldn't take more than a nod of your head to make me throw you down on that mattress and take up where we left off forty-five minutes ago. I want you too damn much to act the platonic friend and it's not fair to you to be anything else."

"No? It appears much fairer than the arrangement you're suggesting," she said, meeting his eyes directly. "And the only one I'm likely to accept. At least I wouldn't be a charity child nibbling at the crumbs from your table. I'd be giving you something you want for your money." Her smile was bittersweet. "Another bargain, not so unlike the first one, except that you've already sampled the merchandise."

His hands tightened on her shoulders. "Will you be quiet?" he grated out through clenched teeth. "You make yourself sound like some kind of prostitute. I'm not setting you up as my weekend mistress because you're too independent to accept help any other way."

"You're quite right you're not," she said

clearly. "But only because I choose not to be. The disposition of my life is my affair and not yours." She pulled away from him. "You have it all planned down to the last detail. College, your stable lifestyle, your very helpful friends. Did it ever occur to you to consult me? I would *love* going to school. Learning new things is exciting and it would be heaven to be surrounded by all those lovely books." She lifted her chin proudly. "But I'm not as ignorant as you seem to think. I may not have had a formal education, but I've worked and studied just the same."

"I know that," he said gruffly. Oh, Lord, now he'd hurt her. Why wouldn't the words come out right? "You're probably better informed than ninety-five percent of the college graduates I've met. But that's not all there is to the educational process. There are dances and football games and lectures and—" He stopped helplessly. How could he convince her when he'd never given a damn about all that stuff himself? But maybe she would. She deserved at least the chance to sample the social side of life. It was his duty to supply that sample. Duty. Lord, he hadn't thought about responsibility and duty since he'd left

Dany and Anthony two years ago. Strange, it wasn't as unpleasant as he'd thought it would be. Not when that duty involved Kate. In time he might even come to enjoy it.

She was gazing at him uncomprehendingly. Dances, football games? It was as if he were speaking a foreign language. What did those things have to do with her? She wasn't a child to be offered amusements such as those. Well, it was evident that Beau thought of her in those terms. She obviously hadn't been far off the mark when she'd described herself as a charity child. Lust may have been an element in Beau's feeling for her but pity was obviously paramount. She felt a slow-burning resentment not unmixed with hurt. She could have tolerated any attitude more easily than that.

"No, thank you," she said dully, her voice as precise as a polite little girl's. "I'm sure that sort of life wouldn't appeal to me."

"How do you know until you've tried it?" he asked roughly. "There's a whole world of experiences out there just waiting for you. You're like a blank blackboard that's never been written upon."

"I'm sorry to disappoint you, but this particular blackboard *has* been written on before. I haven't lived in a convent, you know. In some ways I may have been limited but in others I'll match you experience for experience." She was opening the door and turning to look at him over her shoulder, her eyes bright with tears. "No deal, Beau. You'll just have to find some other charity to patronize." Then she was out the door and climbing lithely down the ladder.

She heard him on the platform above her but she didn't stop at his bellowed, "Kate!"

She'd had enough to contend with for the moment, perhaps forever. She would *not* cry in front of him. It would only substantiate the image he had of her as being some sort of waif to be rescued from a life of crime. She was neither a victim nor an object of pity, damn it.

He was starting down the ladder after her, but she'd almost reached the ground. By the time he reached the bottom of the ladder she'd already faded into the forest.

SEVEN

THE CESSNA WAS safe. She hadn't really thought Despard's men would discover it. Tucked under a green-and-beige camouflage tarpaulin at the edge of the glade, it would have blended perfectly into the landscape from the air. The only way it could have been found was a ground search through the rain forest and Despard's city-bred men weren't equipped for that type of physical undertaking. Still, it was a relief to be sure. She gauged the tires to be certain they hadn't lost any air and was just straightening the tarpaulin back over the wings when she heard a cheerful voice behind her.

"We both had the same idea. Is it ready to go?"

She whirled to face him. "Julio! What are you doing here? I wasn't expecting you until at least late this afternoon."

He shrugged. "Consuello wanted to go into Mariba last night instead of this morning to taste the delights of the sinful city." His dark eyes twinkled. "I tried to convince her that tasting the delights of my gorgeous body would do as well but she insisted she wanted both. A very greedy señora." He moved forward to help her with the tarpaulin. "So we stayed at a hotel near the waterfront and I drifted around to a few bars and kept my ears open. I borrowed her brother's motorcycle to get here after I left Consuello back at her cottage."

"And?"

"The *Searcher* has been impounded. It's been docked at the pier and has a two-man guard."

"And the crew?"

"Seifert and the crew are being held under house arrest at the Black Dragon Inn." Julio's lips twisted, "Very liberal house arrest from what I hear. The authorities aren't taking any chances of offending the Lantry conglomerate even to please Despard. They've been offered both the best Jamaican rum and a few of Alvarez's most talented girls to warm their beds. The authorities are obviously trying to make their time in Castellano as painless as possible. The word is that it may be a long stay."

"Why?"

"Despard is raging like a wild bull; everyone in Mariba has heard about you destroying the coke." He shook his head. "Despard doesn't like losing money and he likes being laughed at even less. Using a little muscle to keep Seifert on ice for a while will help him save face."

Kate bit her lip. "How long?"

Julio shrugged again. "Who knows?" His big hand fell comfortingly on her shoulder. "Don't look so troubled. I told you they're giving them everything they could want or need."

"Everything but their freedom," Kate said soberly. For Daniel that reservation would far outweigh any possible indulgence the authorities would offer him. After his experience in Sedikhan even the lightest confinement would grate unbearably on his nerves. "It's not right they should have to suffer for helping us."

Julio stiffened. "It's not as if they're torturing them with cattle prods, Kate," he said. "And there's not much we can do. There are two armed guards in the hall outside their bedrooms."

"You seem very well informed," Kate said with a grin. "All this you picked up in a bar?"

"I made it my business to be very thorough," Julio replied. "I knew I'd have to have ammunition to convince you how crazy it would be to try to do anything. I know you, Kate."

"Two men in the hallway?" Kate asked, frowning.

Julio nodded. "And even if you could find a way of getting the crew out of the inn, there's no way you could get them here to the plane without being recaptured."

"No, we wouldn't be able to get them to the plane," she agreed absently. "We'd have to take the ship."

He closed his eyes. "*Madre de Dios*, why didn't I realize you'd think of that?" His lids flicked open and he shook his head. "Kate, you can't just hijack a ship and sail it out of the harbor without expecting fireworks from the authorities. You'd never make it out of Castellano territorial waters and they'd charge you with piracy as well as whatever else they've rigged up against you."

"If I'm caught it won't be any worse for me," she said somberly. "You've heard how they treat women prisoners here."

"Which is why you shouldn't risk getting caught. Look, Kate, why don't we just fly Lantry to Santa Isabella and let him use the pressure of his company to get Seifert and his men released?"

Kate shook her head. "No telling how long that would take. I can't let them stay in Mariba if there's any chance of getting them out. They're my responsibility now."

"You can't shoulder the problems of the whole world, Kate." Julio's dark eyes were gentle. "You've got to pick and choose. If we go after Seifert and his crew, we'll have to leave the Cessna. Is rescuing Seifert and the crew more important than giving Jeffrey his new start?"

"No, of course not," Kate said quickly. "We'll just have to find a way of doing both."

He was gazing at her with exasperation mixed with resignation. "What could be simpler?" he asked caustically. "Are we also going to find another cocaine cache for you to burn up if you get bored?"

She frowned at him impatiently. "Don't joke, Julio. This is a very serious problem."

"That's what I'm trying to tell you," he said. "Too serious and too dangerous for us to make the attempt."

She moistened her lips nervously. Julio wasn't going to like this. "Well, actually I thought it would be better to divide up." She held up her hand to stop the protest that was sure to come. "It's the only sensible thing to do, Julio. I'll go to Mariba and work on getting the captain and the crew away from Castellano and you can fly Beau to Santa Isabella and deliver the plane to Jeffrey."

"No," Julio said flatly. "I'm not letting you go to Mariba alone."

"You've got to," Kate said persuasively. "It won't be all that dangerous." She ignored his snort of disbelief and hurried on. "I'll go to Consuello and ask to borrow her brother's motorcycle." She bit her lip thoughtfully. "In a loose jacket and that visored helmet I'll be almost unrecognizable."

"And the guards?" Julio asked. "Are you going to just snap your fingers and make them disappear?"

"I'm not sure. I'll have to think about it. Anyway, after I've released Captain Seifert I'll have him to help me hijack the ship," she said with a grin. "I have an idea he'll be very good at piracy. I can almost see him with an eye patch and a curved scimitar clenched in his teeth."

"If it gets that far," Julio said. "The odds are ninety-nine to one that it won't. I can't let you do it, Kate."

Her smile faded. "You have no choice, Julio," she said quietly. "It's going to be just the way I said. It's the only way we can help the crew *and* Jeffrey."

"No," Julio said firmly.

"Yes," Kate said just as insistently. "If you won't do it for any other reason consider it as payment of a debt." She paused deliberately. "El Salvador, Julio."

"Kate, don't do it." His voice was almost pleading. "Don't make me let you do this."

The battle was won. It was there in his face. She only wished she'd been able to convince him some other way. She smiled with an effort. "Don't worry. Everything is going to work out."

"Is it? I wish I could be as sure. You're going to do it tonight, then?"

She nodded. "There's no use waiting. I may even be able to catch them by surprise."

Julio's curse was very explicit Spanish and rampant with annoyance. "You speak as if you were a commando troop, not one lone woman. This is crazy. *I'm* crazy for letting you do it."

"Let?" Her tone was teasing. "I thought I'd weaned you away from that type of arrogance." His worried frown didn't lighten and she felt a pang of remorse. This was as difficult for her old friend to accept as it would be for her under the same circumstances. "Look, if it will make you feel any better, you can wait until tonight to fly Beau and the plane to Santa Isabella. Once we're on board the *Searcher* and out to sea I'll use the ship's radio to let you know we're safe."

"Safe! You mean until the Guardia Costa—"

"Maybe that won't happen," she interrupted. "Now where did you leave Manuel's motorcycle?"

"At the edge of the forest, about a half-mile from the road that leads to Consuello's village," Julio told her reluctantly. "At least ask Consuello for any help it's possible for her to give you. She's always liked you."

"As long as it doesn't put her in any danger," Kate agreed. She hesitated. "You'd better wait here until almost sundown before going back to the tree house to pick up Beau and bring him to the plane." Her shoulders moved uneasily. "He might be a little difficult about this."

"Because he is a man with all his senses intact," Julio answered caustically. "You wouldn't be able to blackmail him into giving in to this craziness. He doesn't owe you any debts to be called in."

No, it was she who still owed a debt to Beau. A debt he wouldn't let her pay now. He was more inclined to adopt her than make her his mistress at the moment, she thought bitterly. Who would have believed the cynical Beau Lantry she'd met at Alvarez's bar would react like that? Well, if she could free his crew and give him back his ship, it would be a little compensation toward the debt she owed him before she disappeared from his life.

"Sundown," she repeated. "By that time he'll have realized it will be too late to stop me. Tell him I'll see him on Santa Isabella."

Julio's eyes were narrowed on her face. "And will you?"

"Where else would I go?" she asked evasively. Anywhere to escape Beau's pity and generosity. Loving him as she did it would kill her not to meet him on equal terms.

"Kate . . ."

She turned away. "I've got to get going." She impulsively turned back and stood on tiptoe to brush her lips on his cheek. "Take care, Julio."

"*Me* take care?" he asked gruffly. He took her hand in his and fell into step with her. "And you're not getting rid of me so quickly. I'll walk you back to the motorcycle. I left a bundle of clothes I borrowed from Manuel for Lantry tied to the seat." He made a face as he glanced down at the short-sleeved blue shirt he'd had to leave open almost to the waist to accommodate his brawny chest. "I hope they fit him better than they do me."

"I'll be glad of the company," she said with an affectionate smile. They'd traveled so many roads together. It hurt to think this might be the last one for a while. Her hand tightened on Julio's. "By the way, when you leave Castellano, will you take my carousel music box with you?" She laughed a little shakily. "I don't really mind leaving anything else but I'd like to make sure that's safe. You won't forget?"

He shook his head. "I'll remember." He cleared his throat. "I'll deliver it safe and sound to you on Santa Isabella."

Her eyes avoided his as her pace unconsciously quickened. "Yes, you do that," she said lightly. "On Santa Isabella."

As Julio leisurely climbed the ladder to the tree house the rays of the setting sun threw the figure of the man sitting on the platform above him into shadowy silhouette. It was just as well it was twilight, Julio thought. There was something so tense and intimidating about Lantry's immobile form that he had no wish to see that menace any more clearly.

"Where is she?" Lantry's voice was clipped and harsh as Julio swung up on the platform. Now that he was closer he could see the expression on Lantry's face was just as set and harsh.

"Safe," Julio said briefly. *Madre de Dios*, he hoped that was true. He tossed the bundle he was carrying down in front of Lantry. "I borrowed you a change of clothes." He eyed the bare chest of the man in front of him. "They may not fit very well but they'll keep the mosquitoes from eating you alive."

"Where is she?" Beau repeated. The first overpowering relief at the knowledge that Kate was safe was banished by anger. If he had her here he'd shake the living daylights out of her as if she were a beloved but unthinking child who'd stayed away from home too long. Beloved. Yes, she *was* beloved. The hours he'd spent worrying and agonizing since Kate had disappeared into the forest had made that fact very clear to him.

He'd known before, almost from the beginning, but that knowledge had been honed and sharpened by anxiety until it had cut through all the nonessentials. "Damn it, she said the plane was only a short distance from here and she's been gone all day." He was thrusting his arms into an aqua-and-cream flowered shirt with jerky motions. "Didn't it ever occur to her that I might have been a little concerned?" His tone was uneven as he buttoned up the gaudy shirt and shoved the tail into his Levi's shorts. "Of course, there was no reason for me to worry. Only Despard and the police and the Lord know what animals and insects there are in this blasted forest. By the way, are there any tarantulas in this tropical Garden of Eden?" Of all the horrors he'd imagined through the long hours of waiting, the thought of that hairy poisonous monstrosity crawling on Kate's satin skin had been most prevalent.

"I've never seen one," Julio answered cautiously. "And Kate's never mentioned them."

"That doesn't surprise me." The beat-up sandals in the bundle were a little small but beggars couldn't be choosers, Beau told himself. He looked up grimly from fastening the strap. "She tells me she's afraid of all kinds of things but she sure as hell doesn't act like it. Probably poisonous spiders are on the list of things she just blocks out of her mind."

"Maybe," Julio conceded. "Kate's had to do that pretty often over the years. It hasn't been easy for her."

Beau knew that and it filled him with an aching frustration and fury greater than any he'd ever known. Not even when he'd been in the throes of alcoholism had he felt so helpless. He wanted to give her so damn much and she wouldn't let him.

Hell, he'd probably have to make her his mistress before she'd even let him protect her from the insecurity of being without a country. Or he could marry her. He shrugged the tempting thought away in disgust. That's right, reach out and grab what you want. Don't give her a chance to slip away and fall into some other bastard's arms. Even if it's not fair to her, hold on tight and avoid the risk of having her make any comparisons after she's had a few of the advantages she's entitled to. She'd never had a fair shake from anyone else. Why should it start with him? "Well, where is our valiant little tigress now? Still at the plane?"

Julio shook his head, his expression distinctly uneasy. "Not exactly."

Beau went still. "Just what do you mean by 'not exactly'?" he asked with menacing softness.

"Well, not at all actually," Julio said uncomfortably. He released his breath explosively. "She's in Mariba."

"Mariba." Beau felt his heart leap to his throat before an icy chill seemed to freeze the blood in his veins. "That's crazy. She couldn't be in Mariba."

"That's what I told her," Julio agreed ruefully. "As you can see, it didn't do me any good. She's definitely in Mariba."

"Tell me," Beau demanded tersely. My God, Mariba!

Julio obediently related the results of his investigations of the previous night and his conversation with Kate that morning. He studiously avoided looking at Beau's steadily darkening face, but he was no more than half through with his narrative when the other began to swear softly and with great fluency. He finished hurriedly and as he expected at once received the full force of Lantry's anger.

"For God's sake, why didn't you stop her? You should have tied her to the nearest tree if nothing else. Do you *want* to see Despard get his hands on her?"

Julio flinched. "What do you think?" he asked fiercely. "I've known her far longer than you and we've been through more than you could ever dream. She probably saved my life in El Salvador. I told you why I let her go alone."

"Debts, bargains, all of this nobility crap," Beau said wearily. "Between us we'll be lucky if we don't get her killed. It's time we forgot everything but getting her off this damn island in one piece."

Julio's brow creased in a troubled frown. "But I promised—"

"But I didn't," Beau interrupted harshly. "And if you think I'm meekly going to let you fly me out of here and leave her in Mariba alone, you're as crazy as she is."

"I didn't think you would." There was a touch of complacent satisfaction in Julio's smile. "And

I was careful to promise her only that I'd fly the plane to Santa Isabella, not you."

"Very wise, since you wouldn't have been able to keep that particular promise anyway," Beau said crisply. He rose lithely to his feet. "Now what do you say we make tracks for the Cessna?"

"We're going to wait there for her to radio us?"

"Hell, no. As soon as it gets dark you're going to fly me in as close to Mariba harbor as you can manage." His lips twisted. "I hope you're as good a pilot as Kate claims. I don't want you cracking up trying to get low enough for me to jump."

"You're going to jump into the sea and swim to shore?" Julio asked, his eyes widening.

"Unless you have a better idea. Believe me, I'd welcome any other suggestion. I've been in the water so much lately I'm starting to feel as if I'm growing gills."

Julio shook his head. "It's certainly the fastest way to get to Mariba. Probably the only one if you're going to get there in time to do Kate any good." He frowned. "But she's right, you know.

If you go to the inn now, you could blunder in and upset any plan she might have for getting the crew away."

"If she has any plan," Beau said grimly. "In my experience of Kate, she operates ninety percent of the time on impulse power."

"You'd be surprised how often she comes through with flying colors though," Julio said with a grin. "Jeffrey has always said she's a natural."

There was no doubt that Kate was that. Naturally bright, naturally honest, naturally loving. The most beautifully straightforward person he'd ever known and certainly the most maddeningly infuriating one. "I won't go to the inn," he decided reluctantly. "I'll take a chance on Kate getting them away and see what I can do about the ship. Two guards, you say?"

Julio nodded. "That's what I heard."

"Let's hope you heard right. I wouldn't like to receive any unpleasant surprises." He looked ruefully down at the brilliantly flowered shirt he was wearing. "It's going to be hard enough trying to play Errol Flynn in this iridescent garb you've provided me with."

"Manuel likes color," Julio said absently. "God, I wish I could go with you!"

"Someone has to fly the plane and I don't think Kate would appreciate it if you kamikazed the Cessna."

"I guess not," Julio said as he opened the door of the tree house. "I'll be right with you. I promised to get something for Kate."

"The carousel?"

"It was the only thing she wanted."

"It means a lot to her," Beau said. "You go ahead, I'll bring it."

Julio hesitated a moment, his gaze on Beau's face before nodding slowly. "All right. I'll wait down below for you."

It was already dusk in the little room but Beau made his way with instinctive sureness to the rattan chest. A stray wavering ray of sunlight streamed into the dimness, lighting the music box with an elusive radiance. The proud arch of the unicorn's neck, the valiant boldness of the mythical centaur, the perky cheerfulness of the small spotted pony. There was so much of Kate embodied in the whimsical little music box. So much beauty, so much courage, so much . . .

He bent to pick up the music box with painstaking care, feeling his throat tighten painfully. The only treasure she'd wanted to take with her, Julio had said. Well, he wasn't about to let her take this particular treasure and leave him behind. She'd have to learn that wherever she went from now on he'd be beside her. To hell with being fair. He couldn't risk her putting herself into danger like this again. It was going to tear him apart to stand and wait for her to come to the *Searcher*. He'd give her until midnight but no later before he went to the inn. Then he'd be damned if he'd ever let her out of his sight again.

He tucked the music box beneath his arm and moved swiftly toward the door.

EIGHT

"ALL RIGHT, NOW tell me how you managed to get rid of the guards," Daniel demanded as he caught up with Kate's hurrying figure at the corner a block from the inn. "I was happy as hell to see you when you unlocked that hotel room door, but I admit I'm curious."

Kate glanced over her shoulder with an anxious frown. The captain had told the six crew members to split up in twos and follow at half-block intervals to avoid looking suspicious. Yes, there they were.

"Oh, that was my friend Consuello's doing," she said with a grin. "She still had some sedatives from her late husband's medicine chest. We slipped them into a bottle of wine and sent it to the guards with Despard's compliments." She made a face. "I wasn't even sure they'd still be potent enough. They were over two years old."

"Obviously they were." Daniel's teeth flashed white in his bearded face. "They were sleeping like newborn babies when I dragged them into the hotel room." His grin suddenly faded. "But if your little mickey was that old, it might not last long. We'd better hope we have the *Searcher* well away from Castellano by the time they come to and give the alarm."

"We're only a block away from the pier where the ship is docked," Kate said. They were moving swiftly now and were once more in the shadows. "Do you think it's safe to take off my disguise now?"

"Is that what it is?" An amused smile tugged at Daniel's lips as his gaze traveled over Kate's figure, from her shiny scarlet visored helmet to the oversized white linen jacket that came almost to her knees. "I thought it looked a little bizarre. You look a cross between a Martian invader and a Colonel Sanders commercial."

"Colonel Sanders?" A puzzled frown knitted her brow for a moment before she shrugged dismissively. "I may look rather weird but no one can tell who I am. Who would suspect someone dressed like this of any serious shenanigans?"

"You have a point," Daniel said amusedly. "No one could accuse you of keeping a low profile." He suddenly started to chuckle. "Lord, I wish Clancy Donahue could see you. You've got to be the strangest undercover operator on record."

"He wouldn't approve?"

"I didn't say that," Daniel said. "He admires effectiveness no matter how it's cloaked and you were certainly that."

"I was lucky," Kate said soberly.

"Yes, you were," Daniel agreed. "You seem to be very well endowed in that way. So is Beau for that matter. I've seen him pull off some pretty outrageous stunts." He stared at her. "Where *is* Beau?"

She glanced away hurriedly. "On his way to Santa Isabella," she said lightly. "It was my fault you were captured and my responsibility to set you free. I decided not to involve him."

Daniel gave a low whistle. "Do I take it you're doing this without Beau's knowledge? I thought it a little odd he wasn't hovering over you like a protective dragon." He shook his head incredulously. "I can't believe he flew off into the wild blue yonder and left you to your own devices."

"There isn't any reason why he shouldn't." She still wasn't looking at him. "After all, he hasn't any commitment to me."

"Perhaps I would have believed that if I hadn't seen the man jump overboard and swim after you like a guardian dolphin." He suddenly grinned. "He was mad as hell but it didn't stop him from taking the plunge. I'd say an action like that from Beau demonstrates the ultimate in commitment."

"Does it?" she asked huskily. "I really wouldn't know. He's almost a stranger to me." It was true, she assured herself determinedly. Beau *was* a stranger. You could turn and walk away from strangers. This crazy feeling of being joined to him in mind and body in the most intimate of possession was only a mirage that surely would fade away in time. Oh, dear heaven, it had to.

"Tell that to Beau." Daniel's brow lifted skeptically. "I don't think he sees your relationship in quite the same way." His hand suddenly closed on her arm. "The ship is just ahead." He pulled her over into the shadows of the prefab warehouse they were passing. "I hope Julio was right that there are only two guards."

"What do we do?" Kate asked, her eyes on the ship a hundred yards or so ahead. It was a deserted ghost ship in the moonlit darkness. Its usually billowing graceful sails were folded like the wings of a sleeping sea gull. "There doesn't seem to be anyone around."

"What the hell!"

Her eyes flew to Daniel's grim face.

"There's someone on board all right. The auxiliary engines have been started."

"But why would the guards do that?"

"They shouldn't, unless they're so bombed out of their minds they've decided to take it out for a little spin. It wouldn't really surprise me. Those guards back at the hotel were guzzling rum as if it were water."

"Most people do in Castellano," Kate said absently. "Liquor is sometimes a good deal cheaper in the Caribbean."

"Well, they can just keep their damn hands off *my* ship." He stepped back into the street and waved imperiously at the crewmen a short distance away. "Stay here," he said to Kate. "We've got to get on board before they try to maneuver away from the dock and crash into something. I hoped to be a little more subtle and not just charge up the gangplank like the Light Brigade." He shrugged. "Oh well, sometimes there's an element of surprise in the direct approach."

"I'm not going to stay here," Kate said indignantly. "I want to be—"

But Daniel was no longer listening. He and the other crewmen who had joined him were moving almost at a run toward the ship. What did Daniel think he was doing leaving her standing there while he took command? Didn't he realize that getting them out of Mariba was her responsibility? Then she was flying after them and caught up with Daniel just as he was barreling up the gangplank.

He cast her a distinctly annoyed glance. "Get out of here," he hissed. "You've done your part. Luck like yours can't last forever. Beau will strangle me with his bare hands if I let anything happen to you."

"Oh, I don't know." Beau's tone was grim as he stepped out of the shadows of the tall mast near the gangplank. "At the moment I'm more inclined to strangle our sweet Kate myself."

The assault force came to a screeching halt.

"Beau!" Kate said incredulously. "You're not supposed to be here."

Daniel started to chuckle. "I didn't think you'd stay out of the action for long. Where are the guards?"

"Trussed up below in the crew quarters," drawled Beau. "I'd suggest you have them taken ashore and dumped in the nearest alley. We don't want to be accused of kidnapping as well as piracy. Incidentally, I dispatched them with considerably more style than you were displaying. I swam up to the anchor line and climbed it hand over hand à la Errol Flynn. While you, on the other hand, charged up that gangplank with all the tactical finesse of the marines at the Bay of Pigs." Beau shook his head disparagingly. "For an ex-mercenary you looked regrettably unprofessional."

"You're supposed to be with Julio." Kate stepped forward to stand before him. "Damn it, why aren't you, Beau?"

"Be quiet, Kate." There was a thread of steel beneath the softness of Beau's drawl. "You might say I'm a bit upset with you at the moment. I didn't at all appreciate being left behind. I found my jump into the sea from the Cessna less than enjoyable." He ran his hand through his still damp hair. "I'm beginning to feel practically amphibian since you came into my life." His lips tightened. "And I most particularly disliked waiting here wondering what trouble you were getting yourself into at the inn. I've been close to mayhem for the past hour."

"All that was hardly my fault," she said defiantly. "You were supposed to fly to Santa Isabella with Julio."

"So he told me," he grated through his teeth. "I don't take orders as well as your friend Julio. In fact, I don't take orders at all. It's time you learned that, Kate."

She drew a deep shaky breath. She should be used to having him angry with her by now.

There was no reason for the abrasive pain she was feeling at his biting anger.

"If you'll excuse the interruption"—Daniel's tone was laden with irony—"do you suppose it would be all right if we postponed all these re-criminations and got under way? I gather you started the engines, Beau?"

Beau nodded, his gaze still on Kate's visored face. "I thought I'd have everything ready to go when you showed up." His brow knitted in a frown. "What the hell are you doing in that crazy getup? You look like a Hell's Angel reject."

"Daniel said it was more Colonel Sanders," she said. "Who was—"

"It's a disguise," Daniel broke in with exasperation. "Now that we have that settled, may we please sail?"

Beau's brows lifted. "Who's stopping you?" he drawled, a little smile tugging at his lips. "You can't expect me to do absolutely everything. After all, you're the captain, Daniel."

Daniel grimaced before he turned away with a flurry of terse orders that sent his men at a dead run to their stations. "I'll try to contribute my little effort to the cause," he said over his shoulder. "Providing the two of you will get the devil out of my way!" He strode swiftly away, rattling more commands with machine-gun forcefulness.

Beau's gesture had a mocking panache. "You heard the man. I suggest we go to my cabin and let Daniel get on with his work. I have a few words I want to say to you. Very choice words."

She took off her helmet and ruffled her hair wearily. "I'm sure I've heard them before. I think we should help Daniel and the men get the *Searcher* out to sea. I don't want to ruin everything now that we've gotten this far."

"We'd only be in the way." His hand on her elbow was guiding her toward the oak door to the passageway leading below deck. "Daniel has his crew trained to clockwork precision. He tolerates my help on the odd occasion when I insist I want to do my bit, but under pressure like this he'd probably throw us both overboard if we got in his way."

Casting a glance at that dynamic giant on the bridge she could well believe it. There was nothing left of the lazily good-natured man she'd come to know. The vitality and power of total command were surrounding Daniel in an almost visible aura. "Perhaps you're right."

Beau was holding the door for her and she started reluctantly down the stairs. Lord, she didn't want to have a confrontation with Beau right now. The tension and the anxiety of the evening had drained her of everything but a heavy lethargy. Beau, on the other hand, seemed to be as charged with electric energy as ever. "How long will it take to get out of Castellano territorial waters?"

"Not much over a half-hour if we have the wind with us." He opened the door to the cabin, his hand brushing the light switch on the wall. "The auxiliary engines are used principally for maneuvering and docking. They don't give us enough power for any dazzling degree of speed." He shut the door behind them. "And we may need that speed if our little flit is discovered when they come to change the guard on the ship."

"Change the guard?" Kate's eyes widened. Of course they'd change the guard. Not only on the ship but at the inn. "I never thought of that."

"That doesn't surprise me." He took the

helmet she was holding and tossed it carelessly on top of the chest. "It seems to be your modus operandi to leap into trouble without giving it a second thought." His fingers were swiftly unbuttoning the white sport coat she was wearing. "It's a constant source of amazement to me that you've survived as long as you have."

"I had enough to worry about without trying to imagine every little thing that might go wrong," she said defensively. "I managed to do . . ." She broke off and looked down bewilderedly as he finished unbuttoning her coat. "What are you doing?"

"Don't worry, I'm not going to tear your clothes off and rape you." He pulled her coat off her shoulders and down her arms. "Not at the moment anyway. I just want to get you out of this blasted 'disguise.'" The jacket joined the helmet on the chest. "It reminds me what a complete idiot you can be with no effort whatsoever." His fingers were running briskly through her short curls that were crushed from the contact with the helmet and his voice was suddenly uneven. "Such a damn reckless idiot."

His eyes were liquid gold in the hardness of his

face and the tousled bronze lock of hair on his forehead sea-darkened to deep brown. She felt a sudden desire to brush that lock tenderly back into orderliness as a mother would to a dear but untidy child. She hurriedly pulled her gaze away and unconsciously braced herself. She mustn't touch him. He thought her insanely impulsive, but she wasn't foolish enough to risk that. "Then you're well rid of me, aren't you?" she asked with an effort at lightness.

"You seem to be a little thickheaded, Kate." His hands held her shoulders lightly, but she could feel their leashed strength. "I'm not rid of you, nor do I intend to be. Do you think I'd go through all the hell you've put me through if I intended to let you get away from me?" His lips tightened. "No way."

Her chin lifted defiantly. "I thought I'd made my position clear. I don't need your help or your charity. Once out of Castellano territorial waters you can have Daniel drop me off anywhere you like and be on your way. We'll consider the bargain settled."

"Oh, will we?" His voice was dangerously soft. "And what if I decide that you haven't fulfilled the terms of our charming bargain? I was prepared to declare it null and void but if that's the only way I can control you I'll reinstate it in full force. You were to stay with me as long as I wanted you, remember?"

Her lips curved in a bittersweet smile. "But you don't want me. Not really. I'm some kind of rehabilitation project for you. You want to pat me on the head and send me off to Connecticut to—"

"I don't want you?" His eyes were molten gold now. "I told you what you do to me. What does it take to convince you, for heaven's sake?" His face clouded stormily. "Oh, what the hell!"

Then she was in his arms and his lips were on hers in a kiss that was more a hot brand of possession. They touched, devoured, and absorbed with a passion that was devoid of the tenderness he'd shown before. His tongue parted her lips and plunged into the sweet warmth waiting for him beyond. She could feel his hands on her shoulders tightening with unknowing force and the sound he made deep in his throat was a growl of hunger. He tore his lips away and buried them in the curls at her temple. His hands were rubbing and kneading her shoulders with rhythmic urgency and she could hear his breathing grow harsh in her ear. "I want you." His voice was muffled in her hair. "You could arouse me even if I were a eunuch in one of those Mideastern seraglios Daniel was telling me about." His tongue delicately stroked the erratic pulse at her temple. "I sat there on that damn platform all afternoon in a rage. I was worried out of my mind and I was still wanting you. I kept remembering how hot and tight you felt around me and the way your skin shimmered gold in the sunlight. I remembered how you fit me, every curve clinging and caressing like a glove of butter-soft chamois." He drew a deep shuddering breath. "Oh yes, I want you, Kate."

And she wanted him. She was acutely conscious of everything about him—the strength of his lean whipcord muscles, the slight dampness of the aqua-and-cream shirt beneath her cheek, the scent of salt and the dark musk of the aroused male. His voice was dark, too, and rubbed velvet soft against her, causing physical responses that were as natural and beautifully primitive as the swell of the waves beneath the *Searcher*'s hull.

She swayed closer. "Then I'll stay with you," she said simply. "I told you I would. I wasn't backing out of our arrangement. I'll stay with you until you tire of me, just as we agreed."

"Oh, Lordy!" There was amusement, exasperation, and an aching tenderness in the two words. "What am I going to do with you? I always thought I was fairly articulate, but I seem to be lost in a maze of misconceptions where you're concerned. We're right back to square one." He pushed her a little away and his hands cupped her face. All trace of humor had left his expression.

"Listen carefully, Kate, and I'll endeavor to make myself crystal clear. One, I'm not going to get tired of you. Two, the only reason I was sending you to Briarcliff was . . ." The rest of the sentence was lost in the shrieking wail of a siren that sounded as if it were right next to them!

"What the hell!" Beau's hands fell away from her. Then he was bolting out of the cabin and up the stairs. She was right on his heels and by his side by the time he skidded to a stop as they reached Daniel on the bridge.

The wailing shriek was even louder and more piercing out here on the deck but the launch wasn't as close as it sounded, thank heavens. The powerful cone of brilliant light splaying over the dark waves was barely cresting the horizon. Oh, God, the Guardia!

"It sounded so close," she whispered. "I guess it was the reverberation over the water."

"It's close enough," Daniel said grimly. "Damn, if we'd only had ten minutes more!"

"We're that near to international waters?" Beau's eyes were narrowed on the approaching launch.

Daniel nodded. "We've had a stiff wind at our back ever since we left the harbor." He tore his eyes from the launch to glance at Beau. "Well, do we give in to those bastards again?"

Beau shook his head. "Not with Kate aboard. We can't chance it." A reckless grin lit his face. "Do you think you can give them a run for their money until we're past the limit?"

A savage smile of satisfaction touched Daniel's lips. "Watch me!"

They watched him. They stood there on the bridge with the wailing siren surrounding them with its keening cry and the wet spray striking their faces with stinging force. Daniel was at the wheel, his legs parted and braced, his hands maneuvering the ship through the waves as if he were the mythical Charon she'd first compared him to. Dipping and zigzagging, cutting a course of incredible intricacy, their sails billowing in the moonlight as they skimmed over the waves. Kate could feel her heart pound with excitement. It was breathtakingly exhilarating being a part of this strange chase.

The wailing engine-driven launch pursuing them was like a modern-day dragon attempting to catch and devour the graceful entity of this ship from another age. The launch was closer now and there was a bellow in Spanish over a megaphone for them to halt and be boarded. Daniel's answer was a low amused laugh as he executed still another intricate turn.

"I should be frightened," she murmured absently. She wasn't frightened, however; there was only the excitement and this bond of intimate camaraderie that linked the three of them together. "Why aren't they shooting? They're close enough now."

Beau's arm tightened around her waist. "That would mean an international incident. They want to board us and take prisoners. If we don't surrender, they'll probably try to ram and disable us."

"If they can get close enough." Daniel's grin was a gleaming slash in the moonlight. "The *Searcher* has a hell of a lot more maneuverability than the launch. I think we're going to make it."

"Won't they follow us into international waters?" Kate asked. "Castellano doesn't have the reputation of being any too law-abiding."

"Only as long as it's safe," Beau said. "They know the conglomerate would nail them for any infraction. Economic clout is a good deal more effective than diplomacy these days."

It appeared Beau's reasoning was accurate, for no shots were fired from the machine guns they could now clearly discern on the bridge of the launch. But the anger and frustration of the officers were obviously growing with every passing second judging by the enraged threats now issuing through the megaphone.

The launch's movements seemed gross and clumsy in comparison with the *Searcher*, and their engine power was being constantly negated by lack of maneuverability and overcompensation by the man at the helm. It was becoming an amusing game and Daniel was playing it with a verve and daring that was making the crew on the other boat look increasingly foolish.

Kate found herself laughing out loud as Daniel executed a lightning turn that left the launch blundering off in the wrong direction before it could recover and compensate. She looked up to see the same amusement and excitement on Beau's face above her.

"Daniel could make his fortune as a matador," he drawled. "But I don't think our friends on the launch are very appreciative of his skill."

"Well, he's certainly waving a red cape at them," Kate said, laughing. "He's enjoying every minute of it. Just look at his face."

"I'd rather look at yours. You're having almost as much fun as he is." He shook his head ruefully. "And I wanted to send you to the bucolic serenity of the Connecticut countryside."

"Just a little more, lady." Daniel's plea was a

deep velvet croon as his big hands caressed the wheel. "We're almost there."

"How can he tell?" Kate asked curiously.

"He can tell," Beau assured her. "Even without the instruments I think Daniel has a built-in compass and speedometer. It must be something in the genes."

"I just hope that launch is equally well equipped," Kate said, making a face. "They're not going to give up easily."

Then Daniel uttered a yell that was a close relation to a Comanche war whoop and was immediately echoed by the members of the crew.

Kate's heart leaped to her throat. "We made it?"

"You're damn right we made it." Daniel turned to the still pursuing launch and made a jubilant and extremely rude gesture. "Go home, you lousy bastards! You've lost us!"

The officer on the launch evidently concurred because the voice on the megaphone suddenly broke off. Then it resumed with a potent string of curses Kate had heard only in waterfront bars.

"They're falling back but they're still following," Kate said anxiously.

"Stubborn," Beau said. "They'll give up soon. No one likes to admit defeat."

"They don't appear to be very resigned," Kate said. She was shivering, she realized incredulously. She hadn't been at all afraid when the action was going on and the launch had been wailing and bellowing like the bull of Beau's matador simile. Why was she suddenly feeling this sense of cold menace when the actual danger was over and the launch was so silent? They'd even turned off the siren and slowed their engines so they were barely keeping pace with the *Searcher*.

"I don't like it." Daniel's brow was creased with a frown. "I felt a hell of a lot safer when we were keeping them so occupied they didn't have time to think. I don't like it at all."

"What can they do?" Kate asked. "You said they wouldn't try anything once we were in international waters."

"I don't know," Daniel said slowly. "I just don't know."

Beau's arm around her was growing tense. "Go below, Kate."

Her gaze flew to his face. "What?"

"Go below," he said harshly, his eyes fixed on the ominously quiet launch. "And just this once, don't argue with me!"

"But I don't under—"

The silence ended as the launch's engines suddenly roared, propelling the boat toward them with a leap of speed!

"Hell!" Beau was falling to the deck, his arm carrying her with him. She had a glimpse of the launch almost upon them now, but veering to the left.

"Hit the deck!" Daniel's corresponding action followed his command and the members of the crew who hadn't already anticipated the order scrambled to obey.

They were only just in time. A lethal rat-a-tat-tat of bullets peppered the air above them. Dark gaping holes appeared in the white sails and the dark wood of the masts was ruthlessly peeled and splintered. It lasted only a moment and then the launch was veering away and speeding off in the direction of Mariba.

"Is anyone hurt?" Daniel's yell was met with various denials from the men. "The bastards couldn't resist getting in a little farewell salute," he said as he got to his knees. "I have an irresistible urge to go after them and teach them a few manners. How about it, Beau?" There was no answer and Daniel turned. "I said how about—" He broke off as he saw Beau's face, white as marble in the moonlight. "Beau?"

His gaze flew to Kate's limp figure cradled in Beau's arms. Her lashes were dusky shadows on her cheeks, and a thin dark line of blood trickled from the wound at her temple.

NINE

"SHE'S BEEN HIT." Beau's expression was dazed and incredulous. "They've shot Kate!"

Daniel was kneeling beside them in seconds. "She couldn't be hit. They were aiming deliberately high. Even if we'd been standing the bullets would have been over our heads. The sons of bitches just wanted to scare us." He tensed. "Unless one of the bullets ricocheted."

"What the hell difference does it make how it happened?" Beau asked fiercely, his golden eyes wild in his pale face. "Look at her. They've shot her, dammit!" Oh, dear God, a wound in the temple. It must be serious. What if she died?

What if he'd lost her even before they'd really belonged to each other? The thought filled him with such panic and fury he found himself trembling like a child lost in the dark. It was dark. The entire world would be dark now without Kate. "She *can't* die, Daniel. I won't let her die."

Daniel was bending closer, his keen gaze raking the area of the wound. "Don't lose your cool. She doesn't appear to be having any trouble breathing. It's difficult to tell with all that blood but the wound doesn't look like a puncture. She may have been cut by a flying splinter." He frowned. "We need more light. I don't want to move her until we're sure." He called over his shoulder to one of the crewmen hovering close by. "Get me a lantern and a first-aid kit, Jim."

"She's *not* going to die," Beau repeated, his voice harsh with desperation. "There are too many things I have to give her. She's never had anything. I've got to show her how much she means to me."

Daniel's dark eyes were gentle. "You can't buy everything, Beau. Kate's not going to let you subsidize her. She's too independent."

"She's going to have to let me." He gently

tucked a lock of hair behind Kate's ear. "What's the use of having anything if I can't give to Kate? All my life I've had my dear loving relatives and so-called friends clawing and fighting to get their hands on a few shekels of the Lantry Trust. Money's never given me anything I really wanted, but it will now. Because it means I can keep Kate safe and comfortable." He tried to clear the thickness from his throat. "And happy. God, I want Kate to be happy."

"How do you know that money will bring her any more happiness than it has you?" Daniel asked quietly. "I wouldn't say Kate has any materialistic tendencies. On the contrary." The seaman was at his elbow now handing him the dark blue metal box with the red cross on it. "Now we'll see how serious the wound really is. Hold that lantern closer, Jim." He opened the first-aid kit and took out a gauze pad. With infinite care he brushed the blood away from Kate's temple. He didn't look up as he gave a slight sigh of relief. "It's okay. It's just a cut, not even a very deep one. She probably wouldn't even be unconscious if the splinter hadn't struck such a sensitive area as the temple. She should be coming to any time now."

"Are you sure?" Beau looked up, his expression strained and haunted. "She's so damn still."

"I'm as sure as I can be. I'm not a doctor, but I've had quite a bit of experience with wounds."

Yes, Daniel would know, Beau realized, almost dizzy with relief. She was going to be all right. "Thank God!"

Beau was angry with her again, Kate thought uneasily. His voice was harsher than she'd ever heard it. Even through this hazy half-waking mist she was aware of the tension that was vibrating through him like a violin string strung too taut. Her head was throbbing with a dull aching pain. Why was that? She tried to think but everything was a muzzy blur. Oh yes, she'd been struck on the head in the warehouse when they'd burned the cocaine. But that seemed such a long time ago. Why did it still hurt? No, it couldn't be that. The machine gun. She stiffened as memory swept back to her. The ship, the chase, Beau's voice telling her not to argue and go below, the explosive strafe of bullets.

Her eyes flew open. "It wasn't my fault."

"Kate!"

She was too intent to notice the hoarseness of his voice. "It wasn't my fault," she insisted. "I didn't have time to go below." Her brow creased in a cross frown. "Not that I probably would have done it anyway. You have no right to give me orders."

Daniel chuckled. "What did I tell you? Independent as hell."

"She can be as independent as she likes as long as she's all right." Beau's gaze was devouring her in the lantern light and there was such an expression of tenderness and thanksgiving on his face that she caught her breath in wonder. Beau couldn't be angry with her and still look at her like that. "Are you in any pain?"

She shook her head, her eyes still held by that beautifully glowing tenderness. "No, I'm fine. Is everyone else unhurt?"

Daniel nodded. "You were the only casualty. Can you get up?"

"Yes, of course." She made a motion to lever herself upright, which was immediately quelled by Beau's arms tightening about her.

"Lie still," he ordered tersely. "You're sure it's safe for her to move, Daniel?"

Daniel shrugged. "I don't see why not. I told you it's not much more than a scratch."

"Then I'm taking her down to the cabin. Send Jim down with that first-aid kit, will you?" He was standing up with her still cradled in his arms. He drew her protectively close. "I'll take care of her from now on."

Daniel got to his feet and stood facing him. "Any idea where we go from here? Santa Isabella?"

"I haven't decided," Beau said, turning away. "I'll get back to you later. Just get us as far away from Castellano as you can before I get over being thankful she's alive and start wanting to collect a few scalps. I never want her to set eyes on that blasted island again as long as she lives."

He was moving swiftly, carrying her. Her ear was pressed to the silky shirt covering his chest and she could hear the beating of his heart. She felt deliciously fragile in that possessive embrace. Too fragile. It was much too easy to relax and let Beau take charge and she mustn't give in to that momentary weakness. "I can walk. Just let me down and I'll be fine. I wasn't really hurt."

He glanced down at her and his face lit up with a smile so beautiful it warmed her heart. "I know you can, but I don't want to let you go yet. Indulge me a little, sugar."

What was a little independence when he was smiling at her like that? "Okay," she said, nestling her cheek closer to the vital cadence of his heartbeat. She closed her eyes and the steady metronome soothed her into a dreamy lassitude as he carried her down the stairs and laid her carefully on the yielding softness of the bunk. His hands were deft and swift as he undressed her and slipped her beneath the covers. She was so lost in that deliciously lanquid haze that she scarcely heard the soft knock on the door or Beau's invitation to enter.

She felt Beau's hand brush the curls back from her forehead. "Hey, wake up. You can't go to sleep until I've bandaged that cut." The mattress sank beneath his weight as he sat down and she opened her eyes to see him taking the first-aid kit from the slight, wiry crewman. What was his name? Jim, that was it. Then the crewman wasn't there anymore and Beau was bending over her with that same wonderful smile curving his lips.

"This may sting a little," he said as the gauze touched her temple. She inhaled sharply. The antiseptic did sting and it was more than a little. "Damn." His growl was rough with concern. "I'll be through here in just a minute. Hold on, sugar." He was as good as his word and soon the cut was clean and neatly covered with a small square bandage. "That should do it." He closed the first-aid box and fastened the snap lock. "Now you can go to sleep."

"I can?" She was gazing up at him uncertainly. "Aren't you coming to bed?"

He shook his head. "Later maybe. I want to stay awake awhile and make sure you didn't get a concussion when that splinter hit you." His hand ruffled affectionately through her curls again. "I don't know why I'm so worried. You've obviously got a cast-iron skull. It would have to be considering the punishment it's taken lately."

"You could lie down beside me," she said wistfully. Strange how easily you could become used to strong gentle arms holding you lovingly.

He was shaking his head again. "I'm too bushed to risk it. It's been quite a day. I'll just sit here until you go to sleep. I have to go up and talk to Daniel later about our next destination, but I'll drop in and check on you periodically through the night. You won't be nervous alone?"

She shook her head. "I'm used to it. Compared to the rain forest, the *Searcher* is a small planet that has experienced a population explosion."

Beau's grasp tightened. Her entire life must have been a forest of loneliness. Not anymore. He was never going to let her be lonely or vulnerable again. "It slipped my mind that your alter ego is Sheena, the jungle girl." His gaze met hers with sudden gravity. "What shall I tell Daniel about Santa Isabella? Do you want to drop in on Julio and Brenden before we move on?"

"I'd like that very much but it's up to you." She met his gaze steadily. "It's your decision."

"Oh, yes, our bargain. I believe I'm getting exceptionally tired of discussing our bargain." He shrugged. "In any case I'll have a special courier pick up your carousel from Julio and deliver it to you at our next port of call if we don't stop at Santa Isabella."

Her face lit up. "It's safe, then?"

"Of course it's safe. You should know I'd never let anything happen to something that was so special to you." He paused. "Then you're leaving our destination up to me?"

She shrugged. "It doesn't matter where we go. One island is pretty much like another in the Caribbean." She suddenly frowned. "I have to warn you I may prove something of an albatross around your neck. There aren't many ports where a woman without papers is welcomed with open arms. You might be better to go on alone."

"Oh, yes, your nonexistent passport. Well, we'll just have to do something about that, won't we?" He was playing with her fingers and he looked down at them absently as he spoke. "And as I have a fondness for this particular albatross, I have no intention of going on alone." A smile curved his lips. "I don't have your rain forest training, you see. I'd be lonely."

"Would you?" That admission of vulnerability from strong self-assured Beau brought with it a melting tenderness and a breathless spring of hope. "I wouldn't think you'd ever be lonely."

"I've been lonely all my life." He looked from her hand to her eyes. "That's why I need you to stay with me. You promised once you'd take care of me. It amused me at the time, but it doesn't now. I *need* you to take care of me, to guard me from that loneliness. Will you do that?"

Oh, she wanted to. She wanted to give everything to him. She wanted to nurture, protect, and love. Oh yes, above all, love. "Yes, I'll do that," she said softly. She tried to smile but found her lips trembling. "Isn't that the primary duty of a mistress? You'll have to coach me on all the nuances of the role, I'm afraid. But I learn most things quickly."

His face darkened in a troubled frown and he opened his lips to speak. Then he closed them again and once more looked down at her hand he was holding. His thumb rubbed absently at the smoothness of the nail of her index finger. "We're going to have to talk about that," he said. "But not tonight. You need a good night's

sleep to get over that whack you took. We'll discuss it tomorrow. There is one thing you should
know." He still wasn't looking at her. "The situation has changed now. I've found I'm not as
strong as I thought I was where you're concerned. I wanted to play Galahad and Lancelot
for you. Hell, I was even willing to try for that
wimpy Ashley Wilkes."

"Ashley Wilkes?" she asked, puzzled.

"*Gone With the Wind.*" Then, as she continued to look at him in bewilderment, "You missed
that too?" His grin was gently teasing. "That's
one classic you'll have to read. The lady author
had the good taste to write about the glorious
South. I may even make you memorize a passage
or two." The smile faded. "Well, I'm not Galahad or Ashley Wilkes and I can't pretend to be
anything but Beau Lantry." His lips twisted.
"And he's a pretty selfish bastard. I'd like to be
self-sacrificing and martyrish and all that bull,
but it's just not in my makeup. Do you understand?"

"No, not at all. I haven't the faintest idea what
you're talking about."

He muttered a frustrated curse beneath his

breath. "It's just that you're so damn vulnerable," he said harshly. "And you're so god-awful impulsive I'd go crazy worrying every minute what trouble you were going to jump into next. You may think you're a cross between Susan B. Anthony and Joan of Arc, but you could have been killed up on that deck tonight, damn it." He ran his hand through his hair distractedly. "For that matter you could have been killed any number of times in the last days."

"So could you," she protested.

"That's different," he said with a royally arrogant lack of logic. "I can take care of myself." Then as he saw the indignation begin to smolder in her eyes, he shrugged helplessly. "Lord, I did it again. Look, I know you've had to be independent and you've done a hell of a good job raising yourself." He lifted her hand and kissed the palm. "You're a beautiful person, Kate. It's just that I'm not going to be able to stand by and watch you fight your battles all alone." His drawl softened to velvet urgency. "I nearly went crazy when I saw that blood running down your cheek. It scared me, sugar. I don't think I've ever been that frightened in my life." He drew a deep breath and a hint of steel appeared beneath the velvet. "I can't let that happen again. Wimpy Wilkes can go drown himself in his mint juleps for all I care."

Her clear blue eyes were wondering. "I hope you know what you're talking about, for I certainly don't."

"I know you don't," he sighed. "I sound like a first-class passenger on the Disorient Express." He put her hand down and patted it. "Forget it for now. We'll talk about it in the morning. I shouldn't have said anything to upset you. I've probably given you more of a headache than you had already."

"You didn't upset me." He'd confused her, touched her, filled her with hope. "And I don't have a headache. I want to talk right now."

"No," he said firmly. "Go to sleep." Suddenly his eyes flickered gold with mischief. "Would you like me to sing you a lullaby?"

"Would you?" she asked, intrigued.

"Only if I was feeling particularly sadistic. Unfortunately, I can't carry a tune and I've been accused of sounding like a howling bloodhound on the trail. No, upon weighty consideration I think it would be far more relaxing if I told you a bed-time story. Would you like that, little girl?"

"Yes, I think I would." She couldn't remember anyone ever taking the time to perform that cozy little ritual. She settled back more comfortably against the pillows and gazed up at him eagerly. "What story are you going to tell me, Beau?"

"Well, I was considering *Dr. Zhivago*, but that's a little heavy going for a soporific." He tucked the sheet more firmly under her chin. "So I think we'll go for *Gone With the Wind*. Okay, sugar?"

He was so beautiful. His smile was that warm lopsided grin that tugged at her heart and his eyes . . . "*Gone With the Wind* sounds fine."

"It's just as well that I start inundating you with the glory of the South anyway. Now let's see, where shall I start? Once upon a time there was a magnificent plantation called Tara and living within its stately portals was a lovely Southern belle whose name was Scarlett O'Hara—"

"But who was Ashley Wilkes?" she interrupted.

"Hush, I'm coming to that. He's not the hero anyway."

"He's the wimp, right?"

"Right. Now Scarlett was a very spoiled, strong-willed lady who had a yen for our boy Wilkes, who was equally hung up on his cousin Melanie . . ."

The knock on the cabin door was soft and unobtrusive but it aroused her immediately. She sat bolt upright in bed and then snatched the sheet that had fallen to her waist and hugged it to her chin. She glanced instinctively at the smooth unrumpled pillow next to her own. She hadn't really expected to see Beau's bronze head there. She had a vague memory of drifting off to sleep some time after the burning of Atlanta. She'd been conscious of Beau once again tucking the covers around her, then lips as soft as orchid petals brushing her forehead. It had all been so lovely—Beau's half-cynical rendering of his tale of the Southland, the rich low murmur of his drawl, watching the vivid flickering expressions on his lean mobile face. Lovely.

The knock was repeated a little more insistently this time. Beau wouldn't knock, he'd stride in with that royal air of dominance she'd become so accustomed to. She'd been drowsily aware of him coming in several times during the night to check on her as he'd said he would do. "Come in."

Jim, the seaman who'd carried the first-aid kit down to the cabin the night before, had a different burden this morning. He bustled briskly into the cabin carrying a round metal tray with a napkin draped over its contents. "Good morning, Miss Gilbert. I've brought you a bite of breakfast. Mr. Lantry says you're to eat everything on the tray." He set the tray carefully down on the bedside table. "He'd like you to join him and Captain Seifert on the deck as soon as it's convenient. The clothes you were wearing last night have been freshly laundered. I'll bring them right down." He grinned. "I didn't want to chance juggling them with that tray of food. I'm not known for being particularly dexterous. I'd probably end up by having to wash them again."

"I appreciate your laundering them the first time, Jim," she said with an answering smile. "You didn't have to. I could have done it myself. I'm not used to being waited on."

"No trouble," he said breezily as he turned and strode back to the door. "You did us quite a favor springing us from the inn last night. Turnabout is fair play, as they say."

As the door closed behind him, she swung her feet to the floor and wrapped the sheet more tightly around her, tucking the folds beneath her arms. Some favor, she thought wryly as she removed the red-checked napkin covering the tray. They were just lucky that no one had been really hurt on deck last night. She had meant well, but perhaps Beau was right about her impulsiveness. Well, she wasn't going to waste her time in gloomy retrospection when the sun was shining so brightly through the porthole and Beau was waiting for her on deck. She'd savor every moment to the fullest as she'd always done.

And she'd start with this breakfast of bacon and eggs and homemade biscuits that were light as a feather and absolutely heavenly. It seemed that she hadn't eaten in a century or so and it was no chore at all to obey Beau's instructions to eat every bite. Come to think of it, she *hadn't* eaten much in the last few days. She'd had breakfast on the *Searcher* day before yesterday and a little stew at Consuello's cottage before they'd started for Mariba.

Beau couldn't have eaten very much either and he must have appreciated his breakfast as much as she was appreciating hers now. What did he like to eat? she wondered curiously. There were so many things they had yet to learn about each other. The intimacy bred by danger and their explosive physical union had brought them so close it seemed amazing she didn't know the little mundane things about Beau. Well, they'd have time to learn all the things they needed to know now. She couldn't hope that Beau's passion for her would last forever, but from what he'd said last night, he did feel something for her other than desire. Perhaps if she worked very hard and developed the sophistication and poise he was accustomed to in his women he'd begin to feel a little of the love that was beginning to possess every atom of her being.

Forty-five minutes later she gave her glossy curls a last pat and tucked the soft white cotton shirt more firmly into her jeans. She made a face at the reflection in the bathroom mirror. Spick and span she definitely was, but sadly lacking in romance or glamour. Much more cousin Melanie than Beau's Scarlett O'Hara.

Still, when she reached the upper deck and saw Beau leaning indolently against the rail idly talking with Daniel, she didn't feel like sweet wholesome Melanie. She felt as hopelessly romantic and lovesick as any Juliet, Héloise, or Guinevere.

Beau must have changed sometime during the night, for he was wearing close-fitting pale beige jeans. His chocolate brown shirt with sleeves rolled to the elbow made his bronze hair shine even more in contrast. His eyes were more dark hazel than gold today though and there were dark circles beneath them. Hadn't he slept at all?

He frowned disapprovingly as she came toward them. "You've taken off your bandage."

"It got wet in the shower." So much for her spick-and-span allure. All he'd noticed was the lack of that dratted bandage. "I didn't need it anyway. The cut will be better without it." She breathed deeply of the clean salt air. "No self-respecting wound would dare not heal in surroundings like this. Cobalt sea, sapphire sky, and the sunlight . . ." She trailed off searching for a phrase that would describe the sparkling iridescence that was singing through her. "It must have been a morning like this when Noah realized the earth was reborn and sent out his dove."

The frown on Beau's face was superseded by amusement. "First she compares you to Charon and now Noah, Daniel. When she gets to Methuselah you'd better think seriously about shaving off your beard. Evidently it's not projecting the kind of virile image a stud like you would like to present to the world."

Daniel didn't appear equally amused. "Playing ferryman to a bunch of lovesick animals sounds a hell of a lot more appealing than what you had in mind for me," he said with a scowl. "It wouldn't even be legal, damn it. It takes all sorts of special seaman's papers to be qualified for a job like that."

"Then we'll have to move on to plan two," Beau said grimly. "It's got to be legal. If we get someone on board with the right papers and it takes place in American waters . . ."

Kate was looking from one to the other in bewilderment. "What's this all about? I must have missed something along the way."

"Yes, Beau, tell her what it's all about," Daniel

said silkily. "After all, it does concern her. In a minor way of course."

"Shut up, Daniel," Beau growled. "You're not making this any easier." His expression was grave as he turned back to Kate. "We have a small problem. Last night when I came back up on deck to talk to Daniel I had to make a decision about where we were going."

"Yes?"

"I made it. We're about a half-day's journey from our destination now."

"And that is?" she asked, puzzled.

"Santa Isabella." He paused. "First."

"First?"

"Then we're going to continue on to Norfolk, Virginia."

"Virginia!" she echoed. "But that's the United States. Immigration will never let me in without a passport."

"I decided I was tired of batting around the Caribbean. I want to go home," he said quietly. "And you're coming with me just as you agreed."

"But I can't without a—"

"We'll get you a passport, but it may take time

to track down your papers. That's why we're stopping off at Santa Isabella. We need to get all the information out of Brenden we can regarding your birth and the possible whereabouts of your mother. In the meantime I'm not willing to sail around aimlessly like the *Flying Dutchman* waiting for the lawyers to come up with something."

"Then you'll obviously have to go without me," she said, trying to smile.

"The hell I will," he said softly. "Not when there's a way that I can have it all. Daniel can fix it."

"Fix it?"

"Right now we're anchored a mile or so off the coast of Lanique, a U.S. possession. That means we're in American waters. Since Daniel isn't qualified to do the job himself he's going to go ashore, find a justice of the peace or some other official and bring him on board the *Searcher*." He took a deep breath. "To marry us."

"Marry?"

"Marry," he repeated, a trifle nettled. "You obviously view it with very little enthusiasm."

"A very intelligent lady," Daniel said promptly. "Let's forget you ever had this latest attack of insanity, Beau." He made a face. "If it ever got back to Sedikhan I'd played Cupid for love's young dream, it would totally ruin my reputation."

"We're *not* going to forget it," Beau said grimly. "We're going to be married today. Once we're ashore we'd have all sorts of problems tying the knot without papers for Kate. The minute we're married, she's automatically an American citizen and has the protection of both the Lantry name and the Lantry conglomerate. We'll still have trouble with Immigration but it should simplify the whole process enormously."

"That's a pretty drastic solution," Kate said dazedly. "Isn't there any other way around it?"

Daniel opened his lips to speak, but Beau gave him a quelling glance and said quickly, "There's no other way. You made me a promise and this is the only way you can keep it." His lips twisted. "You needn't be so apprehensive. Even conventional marriages seldom last more than a few years these days. It's not as if it has to be forever."

No, it wouldn't be forever, she thought dully. It would only be a convenience in order that Beau could have her at his disposal for as long as it suited him. She mustn't let those words hurt so much.

"I know that," she said quietly. "I was just thinking that in time you may consider it to be more trouble than it's worth."

"I rarely regret any decision I make, regardless of the consequences," he said with a curiously bittersweet smile. "I'll consider it worth it, Kate. You'll do it, then?"

"If that's what you want."

"Very docile," he said mockingly. "Is our Kate so tame now?"

"I don't think I'm particularly meek," she said, meeting his eyes steadily. "I just believe in keeping my word."

"And so do I," he said, his expression softening. "Remember that, Kate. So do I."

His mood was changing from moment to moment with lightning rapidity, she thought dazedly. What did he actually want from her? She'd agreed to what he'd said he wanted, but she was still aware of the current of leashed restlessness and discontent behind that mocking façade.

"Hop to it, Daniel," Beau said. "I want to get it over with as soon as possible." He shrugged. "We'll be married in your cabin. It's as good a place as any."

"No!" Kate said. She'd never thought much about weddings, certainly not her own wedding, but she was experiencing an odd repugnance at the idea of a hurried ceremony rattled off in the confines of Daniel's cabin. The vows they were going to speak may not have any importance to Beau, but they did to her and she wanted to be surrounded by beauty when she said them. "Up here on deck, in the sunlight."

There was a flicker of understanding and tenderness in Beau's eyes. "Why not? Then we can have the entire crew as witnesses. We're going to need all the documentation we can scrounge together."

"I'm on my way," Daniel said, turning away. "I'll have to go down to my cabin first and get my captain's papers and the credentials Clancy provided to prove how respectable I am these days. A justice of the peace isn't precisely the type of official I'm accustomed to using my powers of persuasion on."

Kate took a step forward and placed an impulsive hand on his arm. "You don't really mind, do you, Daniel?"

Daniel's impatient gaze traveled from her hand on his arm to her troubled face. "You bet your sweet . . ." He stopped abruptly as he met her eyes. He was silent a long moment before he smiled with surprising gentleness. "I'll live through it." He patted her hand. "I'll not only be best man, I'll even make the supreme sacrifice for the occasion."

"What's that?"

He glanced ruefully down at his naked muscular chest with its curly thatch of auburn hair. "I'll put on a shirt." He turned away. "But don't expect anything else from me. Enough is enough!" He was almost to the door leading belowdecks when he abruptly turned around again. "Well, maybe one more thing. You're going to need a ring for the ceremony. I know Beau never wears one. Do you have one, Kate?"

She shook her head.

He was taking a large ring of Florentine gold

off his right hand. "Use this one." He tossed it to Beau. "It's my lucky ring though. I want it back."

Kate studied the ring. It was obviously very valuable, aside from the fact that it was fashioned of pure gold. The workmanship was exquisite and the design on the surface very unusual. A rose in full bloom pierced by a sword. "Lucky?"

Daniel nodded. "It was given to me by a powerful Sedikhan sheik I did a favor for once. I didn't know it at the time, but wearing it put me automatically under the sheik's protection. That particular symbol is recognized throughout Sedikhan." His lips twisted. "The revolutionaries I told you about stole the ring after they captured me. When they sold it in the bazaar the buyer took it to the sheik and he contacted Donahue. Together they traced it and that led them to me. After six months in the hellish hotbox I was ready to believe the ring wasn't only lucky but pure magic."

"I can see how you would," Kate said. Magic. This marriage could certainly use any magic as

well as luck the ring could bring them. "Thank
you for letting us use it, Daniel."

"My pleasure." He disappeared down the
stairs.

When she looked back on that strange ceremony it was all a jumble of flickering impres-
sions. The movement of the ship beneath her
feet, the clear warm sunlight bathing everything
in its radiance, the crew in attendance, their
faces surprisingly solemn. The thin, graying justice of the peace, Mr. Carruthers, with his sweet
smile. Daniel, dressed in his cutoff jeans but with
a pristine white shirt buttoned to the throat with
endearing circumspection, the exotic gold ring
being slipped on her finger. Beau's voice low and
oddly husky as he repeated the prescribed vows,
her own voice, faint and far away. It was all
vaguely dreamlike until almost the very end
when Beau turned to face her.

"I'd like to say something," he said softly.
"You're probably not aware of it, but it's become very popular these days for a couple to
make their own vows. I think it started back in

the sixties with the flower children." He smiled gently as he took her hand in his. "I never thought I'd be tempted to follow their example, but here goes." He paused for a long moment and when the words came, they were distinct and clear with a jewel-like richness.

"There are only a few qualities I've ever discovered worth holding onto when I've found them in this tired old world of ours. They are honesty, fidelity, and a loving generosity of the spirit. I've found all of them in you, Kate." His clasp tightened and his golden eyes were liquidly brilliant as they held hers. "I promise to give you my own honesty and fidelity in return. I can't promise to give that same generosity of spirit. That particular quality is so very rare it's almost priceless and I don't know if I even possess it. I *will* give you my strength to protect you, any knowledge and experience I've acquired through the years, and my friendship." He drew a deep shaky breath. "They aren't gifts I give lightly. Will you accept them, Kate?"

"Oh yes." She was so moved she could hardly get the words past the tightness of her throat. "I wasn't expecting this. I don't know what to say in return."

"Nothing," Beau said simply, turning back to Mr. Carruthers. "You don't have to say anything. I just wanted you to know. Let's get on with it."

"There's only a few more lines," the justice said gruffly, hurriedly bending his head over the Bible in his hands.

She scarcely heard the final words that completed the ceremony. She felt as if she were wrapped in the golden warmth of the words Beau had spoken. So beautiful. No words ever had such shining beauty and Beau's gentle kiss at the end of the ritual was also gravely beautiful.

She was vaguely conscious of Beau thanking Mr. Carruthers and an envelope exchanging hands. Then Daniel was inviting them all down to his cabin for a drink before he had the justice taken ashore.

Beau shook his head. "I'm afraid you'll have to excuse us. I need to talk to Kate." He turned to Kate. "Will you come down to the cabin with me?"

She nodded dreamily, barely conscious of his

hand on her elbow propelling her away from the others and down the stairs. The door of the cabin closed behind them and she turned to face him, her eyes still glowing with that soft misty luminance. "What did you want to speak to me about?"

"What?" he asked bemusedly. Then he shook his head as if to clear it. "Do me a favor and don't look at me like that, okay? I had no intention of doing anything but talking when I brought you down here."

"And now?" she asked softly, moving a step closer.

"Now I want to throw you on the bunk and have my wicked way with you."

"I didn't find your way at all wicked before," she said, a little smile tugging at her lips. "I found it very enjoyable. Are you planning on doing it differently this time?"

"Certainly." Beau's eyes were twinkling. "Variety is definitely the spice of life, particularly when it pertains to doing 'it.'" The humor faded from his face. "Listen to me, I'll have you with your clothes off and lying in that bed in a couple of minutes and that's not why we're here. I have to tell you why we went through that ceremony up on deck just now."

"You've already told me," she said, smiling lovingly at him. Her hands began to unbutton her white cotton shirt. "I understand perfectly. You want to go home. I've never really had a home, but I understand the pull is very strong. If that's where you want me, then that's where I'll go." She'd go to the penal colony on Devil's Island if he'd only look at her again as he had on deck while he'd said those beautiful vows. "And you needn't worry that I'll take advantage of you. Whenever you want it dissolved all you have to do is tell me and I'll go away." The words were very hard to get out but they must be said. "And while we're together I'll try not to forget the marriage doesn't really exist. I promise I won't be a Xanthippe."

His eyes were fixed on the lush cleavage revealed by her bra as she shrugged out of her shirt. "Dissolved? What do you mean dis—" He broke off. "Who the hell is Xanthippe?"

"She was Socrates's wife." She was struggling with the back fastener of her bra. "She was very bad-tempered. Socrates said that by living with her he learned to get along with the rest of the world."

"No wonder he was so willing to drink that cup of hemlock," he said absently. He inhaled sharply as the fastener was at last released and she slipped the straps down over her arms and tossed the bra aside. "Why do I get the impression that you're trying to seduce me?"

She stepped still another step closer and began to unbutton his brown shirt. "Perhaps because I am," she said serenely, her naked breasts swaying and heavy against him. The sensitive tips brushing against the cool smoothness of his shirt were already burning and peaking with the readiness that was surging through her entire body. "I've read a few books on the subject. Aggressiveness on the part of the female at times is a very welcome variation." She grinned up at him mischievously. "And you just told me that variety is the spice of life." She pushed the fabric of his shirt apart and rubbed her breasts against him. "You've been the aggressor every time so far. I want my turn."

"Nag, nag, nag," he growled, a dark flush mounting to his cheeks as he instinctively leaned forward to meet the thrust of those tantalizing nipples. "You may not be familiar with women's lib as yet, but heaven help us poor males when you are, Xanthippe."

She slipped the shirt from his shoulders and drew it with painstaking slowness down his arms, brushing against him with every breath and every movement. She could hear his breathing begin to grow labored and the pulse in the hollow of his throat was leaping crazily. How wonderful to know she could have that effect on him. But she wanted to do more, she wanted to give him so much pleasure that he'd be dizzy with it. She loved him so very much. How had it grown so quickly to fill her entire life? Perhaps if she could bring him enough pleasure he would love her, too, if only during the moments of passion. "Have your wicked way with me, Beau. Please."

He shuddered but not with cold. His flesh against her own was burning hot. "Perhaps we could talk later," he said, his palm splaying over her jean-clad bottom. "I think I've lost my train of thought anyway. I think it was going to begin with something about how I realize that you don't know me all that well and how unfair it was of me . . ." He drew a deep breath as he jerked her hips forward so that his iron-hard arousal was pressed boldly against her. "Oh hell, you *do* know me, at least in the Biblical sense. What's one more time?"

One more time. The phrasing made her vaguely uneasy but only for a moment. She was having trouble thinking at all through the haze of heat that was beginning to surround her. Beau's hands were working swiftly at the fastener of her jeans and she was suddenly confused about who was seducing whom. "What about my turn?"

"Sometime when I haven't been without you for a century or so," he said thickly. "But I'll be magnanimous and let you help." He pushed her away. "It will be quicker if we both take off our own clothes anyway." He patted her bottom briskly. "Hurry."

She tried, as much as fumbling fingers and curious eyes could hurry. She wanted to watch him as he undressed with that swift athletic economy of movement. She hadn't gotten a chance to look her fill that morning at the pool. He was all power and lithe supple muscle, his buttocks hard and tight, the line of his thighs and calves developed to whipcord toughness. She slipped her tennis shoes off and left them with the rest of her clothes as she stood and gazed at him admiringly.

"You have very nice legs," she said dreamily. "Is that from skating?"

He glanced up from slipping his own shoes off, his lips twitching. "Thank you. I suppose that exercise had something to do with my marvelous physique. You, on the other hand, have utterly fantastic breasts and I'm quite sure you did nothing at all to deserve that boon." He shook his head with mock mournfulness. "Most unfair." He took her hand and led her to the bunk. "However, I'm sure that a little well-directed calisthenics can only improve them. Let's see, shall we?"

"Whatever you like," she said, her lashes demurely veiling the mischief in her eyes. "I wouldn't want to be accused of being uncooperative. You've already convinced me I'm a nag."

"Whatever I like," he repeated softly. "It will be what you like too, Kate. I promise." As she would have sunk down upon the bed he stopped her with his hand on her arm. "No, not that way. Something different, remember?" He sat down on the edge of the bed and drew her down on his lap. "Something beautifully, excitingly different."

It was already different. The hardness of muscle and bone against her cushioned softness, the flickering heat in Beau's golden eyes, the urgent arousal pressing against her thigh. Different.

"It's always been beautifully exciting, Beau," she said laying her head confidingly on his chest. His heart was pounding erratically against her ear, but his hand was infinitely gentle as it stroked her curls. "It's as if you're giving me wonderfully precious gifts every time."

His laugh was a husky chuckle beneath her ear. "You've certainly got an original way of expressing yourself." He ruffled her hair. "It's definitely mutual, little Sheba. It would be highway robbery to charge you one hundred twenty talents for this." He was swinging her around to face him, positioning her legs on either side of his hips on the bed. "Though I'll industriously endeavor to prove I'm worth every single talent." He drew her close, his hands rubbing up and down on her back in lazy circles. "Isn't this nice?" he whispered in her ear. "I can touch almost every part of you." He made a minute adjustment and he was suddenly pressing against the center of her womanhood. "And you can touch me."

Her hands clutched spasmodically at his shoulders. "Yes, very nice," she said faintly. Nice wasn't the word for it. She had never felt more vulnerable in her life and there was a liquid burning that was becoming a throbbing ache deep within her. "Do you suppose we could get on with more in-depth touching?"

"When this is so sweet?" His drawl was boyishly playful. "And we haven't even started your exercise regimen yet." One hand cupped her bottom, retaining the contact while the other hand moved to her shoulder and pushed her body backward so that her spine was arched and her full ripe breasts were offered temptingly. "That's better," he said. "Now just keep that position, sugar. Do you feel the tension? Maintaining the tension is very important in any exercise curriculum, you know."

"No, I didn't know," she said faintly. "And yes, I do feel the tension." The position was almost unbearably erotic. The slight strain of the muscles in the small of the back and hips, the vulnerability of her open thighs and Beau's almost blinding sensual gaze on her breasts. "Beau?"

"You want more?" His bronze head was bending with maddening slowness until his lips were only a breath away from the pink crest of her breast. "So do I." His lips enveloped her nipple with teasing delicacy while his hand dropped from her shoulder to her other breast and began a rhythmic massage that caused a shudder to ripple through her. "Keep the tension, love," he muttered, his tongue licking the pink aureole teasingly. "It will make it better for you. I want it to be so good for you, Kate."

She was trying but it was becoming increasingly difficult when each muscle and bone in her body felt as if it were melting away like molten lava. Her breath was coming in little gasps and she instinctively tried to clench, hold, but there was nothing.

"Not yet." Then as her back arched in the

tension he was demanding, his lips and hands accelerated their rhythmic pressure. "That's the way." His voice was a low velvet croon. "Sweet, soft Kate." His hands dropped away from her breasts to slide around her, one cupping her buttocks, the other at the small of her back, arching her even more. "Now, we'll do a little of that in-depth touching you were talking about. But slowly, very slowly." His lips enveloped her breast with strong suction while his hand on her bottom began to push her slowly forward. His hand arching her back prevented her from thrusting forward and wresting control from him. A little, then a little more, hotness, fullness, but never enough. Her breasts were heavy and swollen, his tongue and teeth an aching torment. He was moving so damn slowly! She felt herself clench around him trying to hold him, invite him, entice him. She heard him gasp and give a low shaky laugh. "Oh, that was sweet. But don't do it again, love. I don't think I could take it."

"What do you think about me?" she said, closing her eyes as his hand lazily caressed her back before resuming the pressure against her bottom. "I can't stand this!"

"Yes, you can." His lips switched to her other breast to give it equal homage. "We're almost home, Kate." He suddenly pushed hard and strong and was filling her completely. She gave a low guttural moan of infinite satisfaction. "What a lovely sound." His breathing was becoming labored. "Let's hear it again." He jerked her up and forward and this time her gasp was a keening cry of need.

He lifted his head from her breasts and wrapped his arms around her. His lips were buried in the curls at her temple. "Oh, Lord, this is wonderful. I never knew anything could be so fantastic. And it couldn't with anyone else." His hands were caressing her naked back with loving gentleness. His lips covered hers and his tongue thrust deep and probing. He raised his head and drew in a deep breath as if his lungs were starved of oxygen. "Only you, Kate. Only with you."

He didn't wait for her to answer. His hands were on her hips, moving her, thrusting, penetrating so deeply it made her gasp. It was so wild and sweet and hot that she moved from peak to peak with scarcely a breath in between. It was unbelievable that any sensation this exquisite could be sustained for so long but somehow Beau accomplished the impossible. It seemed an eon later that the final peak was reached and they collapsed back on the bed in a state of euphorically languid exhaustion.

Sleep followed as inevitably as a rainbow after a sunlit storm. Gentle sleep, held securely within strong possessive arms. So wonderful to be held so lovingly with her ear pressed to Beau's heart, hearing the steady vital cadence and knowing she could make that metronome erupt into rapid explosiveness at a single touch. But not now. Now it was enough to know they had all the time in the world to enjoy that magical intimacy. Beau had looked so tired and strained up on deck. He needed to rest. Her arms unconsciously tightened around him. Rest, love, while I guard you from the world. Lay down your arms. Sleep, and I will shelter you from all loneliness and . . .

"Kate, wake up."

She *was* awake. She was just enjoying being stroked with such affectionate tenderness. She opened her eyes drowsily. He was sitting on the side of the bed completely dressed, no longer vulnerable but still every bit as beloved. Still, she felt a little ripple of disappointment. "I wanted to take care of you."

"What?" He frowned. "I think you're still half asleep. We'll be docking in Santa Isabella soon and we need to talk."

He handed her a white toweling robe that looked vaguely familiar. Oh yes, she'd worn it that first night on the *Searcher*. It seemed such a long time ago. Docking so soon? They must have slept for longer than she'd thought. The rays streaming through the porthole of the cabin were much longer and weaker now. It must be quite late in the afternoon.

"You said you wanted to talk before," she said, giving him an impish grin as she slipped her arms into the sleeves of the terry robe and tied the sash about her waist. "We never appear to get around to it, do we? Something always seems to interfere. First, the Guardia, then my wound, then—"

"We've run out of time," he interrupted with a soberness that made her vaguely uneasy. "We have no choice now." His smile was mirthless. "I wish to heaven we did."

She moistened her lips nervously. "So talk. I'm listening."

He stared at her helplessly as if wondering where to begin before letting his breath out in an explosive sigh. "Oh hell, there's no use beating around the bush. As soon as I get the preliminary immigration red tape out of the way, I'm sending you to Briarcliff to Anthony and Dany."

"Sending—" Her eyes were wide and shocked in her suddenly pale face.

"You'll be much better off with them. There are things they can give you, things you deserve to have." He was speaking rapidly, his gaze fastened somewhere over her left shoulder. "They're great people and you'll learn to love it there."

She shook her head dazedly. "We've talked about this before. I told you there's no possibility I'd go to Connecticut. I thought you understood that."

"I understand that you don't know what's good for you," he said gruffly. "You'd rather wander around the world as my mistress because of that blasted streak of independence. Well, you're my wife now. You have a claim on me. There's no reason for you not to take advantage of a few of the fringe benefits."

"Isn't there?" she asked dully. The shock was ebbing, leaving only pain. "I thought you said the marriage was for your benefit. Does that mean you're going to go sailing off on your merry way as soon as you put me on a plane for Briarcliff?"

"No!" The denial was swift and immediate. "I told you the situation had changed. I'll be around. Do you think I could just let you go now that I know how trouble seems to follow you?"

He'd be around. Of course he would. He couldn't let his little waif wander around without his protection. He'd promised to give her his strength, knowledge, and experience. But she mustn't think of those gravely beautiful words. They hurt too much. After all, he hadn't promised her love. She hadn't dared wish for that and he'd been very careful not to promise her anything he couldn't deliver. He was too honest for that. But not too honest to use a little subterfuge to get his own way. Her gaze slipped away from his face. "You lied to me." Her eyes were stinging with tears she refused to let fall. "You weren't honest with me, Beau."

"I know it," he said harshly. "Do you think I don't? It was necessary. It was for your own good, damn it."

"Who gave you the right to decide what was good or bad for me?" Her voice was shaking. "Who the hell gave you that right, Beau?"

"No one gave it to me. I took it." His gaze at last returned to her face. "And I'd do it again, Kate. If it meant keeping you safe, you can bet there'd be absolutely no question about it." He ran his fingers through his hair. "Now, for God's sake, be sensible."

"Sensible!" Oh, Lord, her voice was close to breaking. *She* was so close to breaking. She had to get rid of him. Pity was already the paramount emotion he felt for her and she'd be damned if she'd add fuel to that pity by dissolving into tears. She carefully steadied her voice. "I'll try to be sensible, Beau." Her smile was shaky. "I'll have to think about it. You'll have to give me a little time."

"Kate." His hand reached out impulsively as if

to touch her hair but paused in midair. "Oh, hell!" he said with soft violence. He stood up. "You'd better get dressed. We should be docking any time now." He was striding swiftly toward the door. "I'll see you up on deck."

The door slammed behind him and her pent-up breath released in a rush. She had a little while now to let the pain flow over her and come to grips with it. She mustn't cry though. Her eyes mustn't be red when she joined him on deck. She'd just sit here and soon she'd be strong enough to face him again. See, she was better already. Her throat wasn't nearly as tight and if she kept her mind perfectly blank she'd be able to keep it that way.

Unfortunately for her excellent intentions, her gaze fell on the strange and beautiful ring still on her finger. The rose and the sword. Pure magic, Daniel had called it. But the magic hadn't lasted very long, had it? Her hand cradled the ring lovingly, not even aware of the slow desolate tears that began to rain down her cheeks.

TEN

"I FORGOT TO give this back to you," Kate said quietly, extending the ring to Daniel. "It was very kind of you to lend it to us."

Daniel's large hand closed on the ring and thrust it carelessly on his finger. "I thought so." He grinned. "I've never been a best man before. Actually, the entire business was less embarrassing than I thought it would be." He leaned back and stretched his bare powerful legs as far as was possible in the confines of the backseat of a taxi. "Toward the end of the ceremony I was beginning to feel so solemn and upright it was positively nauseating. I wouldn't want to do it too often, however, or I'd probably become just as boringly responsible as Beau's getting."

Kate was staring blindly out the window of the taxi. Responsible. The word cut with the sharpness of a scimitar. Not love or even desire, responsibility. "No, you wouldn't want to do that," she said drearily. "Beau has enough of that particular virtue for all of us." She could feel Daniel's gaze on her profile sharpen and tried to rouse herself. "Where are we going? I'm afraid I didn't pay any attention to what you told the driver when we got into the cab."

"The village. It's a very exclusive resort on the other side of the island. According to Carruthers, besides the central hotel it has a number of private bungalows situated on the beach. Beau told me to take you there and get you settled while he went to see your friend Brenden and tried to get a line on your birth records. He said to tell you he'd make arrangements for you to see Brenden and Rodriguez tomorrow. In the meantime he thought you might want to replenish your wardrobe at the shops in the main hotel. He made a call and arranged for them to bill the Lantry conglomerate for anything you decided you wanted."

"How very generous of him," Kate said ironically. But then she'd known he'd be generous, at least monetarily. She only wished that generosity could have been more emotional than financial. No, she wasn't being fair. He'd shown her tenderness, laughter, passion, everything but love. It wasn't his fault he didn't have that to give her. Just as it wasn't her fault she couldn't accept the pity he offered in its place. "I won't need very much. Just a few changes of clothes."

She must be careful not to buy too much. Those shops would probably be exorbitantly expensive and it would take forever to pay Beau back after she left him. That she *would* leave him wasn't even in question. It was inevitable, and it must be soon. Very soon. She had to escape so she could begin to heal.

"Don't be too modest in your demands." Daniel's eyes were twinkling. "You're a married woman now. There's such a thing as community property, you know."

"If you mean to imply Beau owes me something just because of that ceremony we went

through, that's utterly ridiculous," Kate said
tautly. "Beau said that too. Nothing's changed
just because of a few words that were spoken
over us. I'm still me, with my own obligations
and duties. And Beau"—her voice was becoming maddeningly husky—"Beau is still Beau."
Golden-eyed recklessness, strength, and tenderness. Beau.

There was a moment of silence. "I think I de-
tect a note of discord in honeymoon heaven,"
Daniel said slowly. "I noticed Beau was a little
uptight but I thought it was because he was impatient with all that red tape he's having to un-
wind. Dealing with bureaucratic types isn't his
favorite pastime." He paused. "But it's more
than that, isn't it?"

She kept her eyes firmly fixed on the window.
"Yes, it's more than that." She tried to smile.
"I'm afraid your ordeal was all for nothing,
Daniel. This is one marriage that was over be-
fore it started."

"Uh-uh." The negative was so firm it brought
her startled gaze back to his face. "I detest
wasted effort. It's a little idiosyncrasy of mine.
After I compromised my image so drastically

there's no way I'm going to let you untie the knot without good reason." His voice softened. "I saw your face after Beau had put my ring on your finger. You were glowing like a Sedikhan sunrise."

"That has nothing to do with it," she said shakily. "You heard Beau. It was only a convenience to get me past Immigration."

"A marriage of convenience?" Daniel scoffed. "Not likely, Kate. They went out with jousts and suits of armor. Beau wouldn't be involved with an idiocy like that."

"You obviously don't know him as well as you think you do." Her smile was sadly sweet. "That's exactly the kind of idiocy that Beau would become involved with. He's out to save the poor little orphan at any cost. He married me because he thought that was the only way I'd let him take care of me." She blinked furiously to keep the tears at bay. "Well, he was wrong. He should have known that blasted ceremony wouldn't make any difference."

"Oh, Lord!" Daniel groaned, closing his eyes. "Maybe Beau's an idiot after all. He certainly seems to be guilty of a remarkable lack of communication. . . ." His lids flicked open and there was a glint of determination in their depths. "Okay, it's obviously up to old parson Daniel to clear the decks."

A smile tugged at the corner of her lips at the outrageously inept comparison. "I appreciate your wanting to help, but it's not your concern, Daniel." Those blasted tears were welling again. "There's nothing anyone can do."

"You're going to cry," Daniel accused with exasperation. "Now I'm going to have a wishy-washy prima donna on my hands."

"I'm *not* going to cry," she said indignantly. "And I'm not wishy-washy."

"I didn't think you were, but I'm beginning to change my mind. Whatever happened to the girl who broke me out of the Black Dragon Inn? I might have criticized your impulsiveness but not your lack of determination." He shook his head in disgust. "You and Beau are quite a pair."

"What do you want me to do?" she asked fiercely. "I can't make Beau love me and I don't want his damn pity."

"Pity!" He shook his head "Muddle-headed as well as wishy-washy. Look, Kate, men don't marry because they feel sorry for a woman. Hell, I never thought I'd see the day when Beau would marry at all. Didn't it occur to you it would take something pretty monumental to make Beau give up his freedom after all these years?"

"I told you why he did it. He felt sorry—"

"Bull," Daniel interrupted. "He's crazy about you. I've never seen a man so besotted in my life."

"He wants me," she corrected huskily. "I would have settled for that. I know it's more difficult for men to love than it is for women." She lifted her chin. "But I won't accept any relationship where I can't at least stand upon equal terms."

"Equal terms," Daniel repeated. "Yet you clearly don't have any conception of equality in the man-woman relationship itself. Where the devil did you get the idea men were short-changed in the emotional department?"

"But Jeffrey and Julio always—"

"All men aren't Jeffrey and Julio." Daniel was definitely annoyed. "I'd match my emotional sensitivity against yours any day. Beau *loves* you, damn it."

She shook her head. "He never said he loved

me. He promised me everything else, but not that."

"Are declarations so important? Maybe Beau has trouble saying those words. How do I know?" He shrugged. "All I know is what I saw in his face that night he thought the Guardia had killed you. And it sure as hell wasn't pity, Kate."

"It wasn't?" Oh, God, he was probably mistaken. It was too wonderful to be true. But what if he wasn't? What if Beau actually loved her? "You're sure, Daniel?"

She sounded like an uncertain little girl and the hardness softened and then faded entirely from Daniel's face. His large hand covered hers. "I'm sure," he said gently. "I don't see how you could be so blind you couldn't see it for yourself. How many men would get themselves embroiled in the kind of brouhahas you've been inciting all over the Caribbean for someone they just felt sorry for?" He grinned. "It should have been a dead giveaway when he jumped into the sea and paddled after you like your faithful dog Tray."

"He loves me?" she whispered, her eyes aglow with wonder.

"He loves you," Daniel repeated firmly. "Perhaps it's not surprising the two of you are having trouble communicating. You were both cannoned into a relationship as if you were shot from a howitzer. You haven't had a chance to learn each other."

No, only to love each other. But if Daniel was right, they would have all the time in the world now for that other learning process. *If* he was right. She frowned anxiously. "It doesn't make sense. Why would he want to send me away if he loves me?"

"Why don't you ask him?" Daniel asked. "And when you do, remember you're dealing from strength. You impress me as a lady who's more than capable of getting things done once you set your mind on something. Do you want this marriage to work?"

"Yes. Oh yes," she said softly.

"Then I suggest you set about assuring that it will." He winked. "Just pretend that Beau is a cocaine cache to be snatched or an imprisoned crew to be rescued. That should make it a piece of cake."

Her hand tightened on his. "I'll do that." She would just take a deep breath and do what had to be done in this most important venture of her life. "Will you be there to give me a little moral support?"

He shook his head. "You don't need me. I'd just be in the way." He looked down at the gold ring on his finger. "Besides, I have a few loose ends to wind up before I go back to Sedikhan."

"You're definitely returning to your very dangerous Mr. Donahue then?" she asked lightly.

"Why not? I have an idea Beau is going to turn into a very boring solid citizen. That will take all the fun out of being captain of the *Searcher*." His smile was a little whimsical. "Remember I told you we were both searching for something? I've found what I was looking for."

"Everything you were searching for?" she probed gently.

For an instant there was a flicker of something lost and vulnerable in the depths of those snapping navy blue eyes. "Perhaps not everything, but for now it will have to be enough." Then that vulnerability was gone and he grinned. "Well, at least Beau has found it all. Now all you have to do is get him to admit it."

It sounded so easy. She moistened her lips

nervously as she thought just how important that confrontation to come was going to be. Oh, please, let Daniel be right. Please let her be able to make Beau say the words of commitment that would keep them together for the rest of their lives. No, she mustn't let herself have any doubts. She lifted her chin valiantly. "No problem. As you said, it will be a piece of cake."

The sun was going down in an explosion of glorious color, appearing to drain the sea of its own richness in contrast. On this deserted sand dune where she was standing Kate could feel the breeze, warm and soft touching her cheeks. That was also a contrast for there was nothing soft and warm in the violent beauty of the sunset. It bathed the white sand dunes in a fiery glow, and even the towering modernistic hotel in the distance appeared as a blazing sword against the horizon.

Sword. That brought back the memory of the intricately carved sword piercing the rose in Daniel's exotic ring. Magic. She must believe with all her heart in that magic now.

"What the devil are you doing this far from the hotel?" Beau's rough voice behind her made her heart leap. "A lone woman on a deserted beach is an open invitation."

She turned to face him. The fiery glare turned his bronze face to teak and lent the texture of his black jeans and shirt an illusion of velvetlike depth. "I see you got the note I left at the bungalow. That's exactly what I wanted to convey," she said lightly. "An invitation."

"That's fairly obvious." The roughness of his voice deepened to huskiness as his gaze wandered over her lingeringly. Lord, she was beautiful. The loose white silky beach dress she was wearing reminded him vaguely of the caftan she'd worn that night in the rain forest except for the low cut of the square neckline. Her throat looked graceful and infinitely vulnerable as it rose from the gown and her face was lit with a glowing eagerness that caused his throat to tighten helplessly. So sweet. He glanced away hurriedly. "You've been shopping."

"I've spent a great deal of your money." She stepped deliberately closer and into his line of vision. "And I have no intention of paying it back.

Daniel says it's all community property." She smiled. "Did you know community means companionship and mutual sharing? I looked it up when I got to the hotel. I like that idea very much."

There was a flicker of surprise in Beau's eyes. "I don't want you to pay it back," he said gruffly. "I told you on the ship you have a claim on me now. I'm glad you're being so sensible. Does this mean you're not going to put up a fight about going to Briarcliff?"

"I have no intention of objecting to going anywhere you want me to go." She paused deliberately. "I told you how much I loved words. There are some very beautiful ones in the Bible that express how I feel about that. 'Entreat me not to leave you and to return from following after you, for where you go, I will go, and where you lodge, I will lodge; your people shall be my people, and your God, my God; where you die, I will die and there will I be buried.'"

She met his eyes with a simple directness that caused his heart to turn over in his breast. "I mean every word, Beau. I'll go anywhere, be anything you want me to be as long as we do it together." She smiled faintly as she repeated softly. "Always together. Go with me to Briarcliff and stay by my side and you'll have no trouble keeping me there."

"Kate . . ." He took an impulsive step toward her with an instinct as old as the words she'd just quoted. Then he stepped back and his arms fell helplessly to his sides without touching her. "I told you I'd be there to keep an eye on you."

"So avuncular?" She shook her head. "That's not good enough, Beau. I want a husband, not a guardian."

"You don't know what you want," he said, his expression strained and taut. "Your head's full of dreams of Romeo and Juliet and the world well lost for love. And I sure as hell didn't make it any easier by taking you to bed and giving you your first taste of sex. There are things you deserve, things you *need* and it's not fair to let you think I'm the only one who can give them to you. I hope when you've gained a little experience you'll still want me but . . ." He trailed off, running his hand distractedly through his bronze hair. "Lord, I hope that, Kate!"

"I will," she said softly. "There's not going to

be a moment for the rest of my life when I won't want you." Then as he opened his lips to speak, she held up her hand. "Don't say it. I *do* know, blast it. I don't deny I have certain ideals and dreams. Everyone has dreams. That doesn't mean I'm some kind of Peter Pan existing in Never Never Land. I've lived a rough, hard life, Beau. If I don't know the difference between reality and fantasy now, I never will."

"It's because you've had such a hard life that I shouldn't take advantage of you." Beau's lips were set in a stubborn line. "We'll do it my way, Kate."

"I don't think so." There was a hint of steel beneath the sweetness in her voice. "This is too important for me to give in to your idiotic sense of chivalry."

"Chivalry!"

He sounded so outraged that she had to smile. "Sorry. I didn't mean to insult you but I'm afraid you're terribly prone to that hopelessly outmoded code. The signs are unmistakable to someone who's spent most of her childhood with a man who steered his life by dreams and concepts from another age. You're the one who lives in Never Never Land. When I asked Daniel why you were sending me away, he said to ask you." She shook her head. "But I don't have to do that. I've been doing quite a bit of thinking and I realized I may not know a good deal about your mental processes, but I do know that you're far worse than any Lancelot or Galahad." She wrinkled her nose impishly at him. "You're even worse than Ashley Wilkes."

"Now that's an arrant falsehood," Beau said. There was a flicker of amusement in the depths of his eyes. "I won't let you malign me in that fashion, Kate."

"I'll take back Wilkes," she granted. "But the rest is carved in stone. You're a throwback, Beau. Jeffrey was avant-garde in comparison. Well, you can just practice throwing your cloak on someone else's mud puddles. I can take care of myself."

Beau's golden eyes were suddenly glowing with mischief. "Then can I talk you into tossing your cloak on my puddle? I've developed a violent aversion to bodies of water of any description lately."

"Any time." She smiled with loving sweetness.

Her cloak, her body, her heart. "Just say the word."

"I wish you wouldn't look at me like that," he said with a rueful shake of his head. "It makes me feel very strange."

"Good," she said. "I want you to feel strange and off balance. It makes my position that much stronger. Not that I need it. Daniel says I'm dealing from strength."

"Daniel seems to have had quite a bit to say. I'm curious to know what he considered your ace in the hole."

She took a deep breath. "The fact that you love me," she said in a little rush.

There was a flicker of undefinable emotion in Beau's face. "Do I?"

She nodded. "Yes, Daniel says you do. And I've decided he's right. You *do* love me, Beau." Her lips were trembling as she tried to smile. "Do you know why I'm so sure?"

"No." His eyes were fixed compulsively on her face.

"Because there's no way I could love you this much and not be loved even a little bit in return," she said haltingly. "I feel so close to you I think I'd know it if you were rejecting me either consciously or subconsciously." She made a helpless little gesture with one hand. "I'd *know*, Beau."

"You've known me for only a few days," Beau said hoarsely. "I was your first lover. You can't be sure you love me. Six months from now there may be someone else."

"My first lover, my last lover, my only lover." Her eyes were glowing softly. "Sometimes it must happen like that. First the loving and then the learning. Perhaps it's better that way. Just think of everything we have to look forward to experiencing together." She took a step closer and her hands reached up to cradle his cheeks in her palms. "Say it, Beau."

"No, it's not fair." His face was harsh with strain. "I won't use that kind of bribery on you, Kate."

"Bribery?" she repeated, startled.

"Love can be used as bribery." His lips twisted bitterly. "Believe me, I know. I can't tell you how many times I've had sundry uncles, aunts, and cousins dangle that carrot in front of my nose. 'We *love* you, Beau. Tell the nice judge you want to stay with us,' or, 'We *love* you but we *do* need all that lovely money so we can be comfortable, don't we?' Some people seem to think that saying those words gives them the right to demand almost anything in return." He shrugged wearily. "Hell, sometimes it nearly worked. I wanted to belong somewhere so badly that I came pretty close to believing one or two of them." His eyes were grave. "I won't use those tactics on you, Kate. You don't owe me anything."

She felt a rush of joy. He did love her! Now only the last shadows of the past were left to be cleared away and to do that she had to make him say the words. "You're not Uncle George, Beau, and I'm certainly not a little boy desperately wanting a family. I'm a woman who loves you." She frowned. "Or maybe you think I'm trying to use that same kind of pressure on you."

"No, of course not," he denied quickly. "I know you wouldn't ever—" He broke off as he met her quiet smile of satisfaction. "It's not the same thing."

"Isn't it? I think it is. Something very wonderful and special has happened to us and the past has nothing to do with it. I'm not letting my background interfere and neither should you, Beau. I don't want you to be chivalrous or even be what you deem as 'fair' to me. All I want is for you to love me. The rest will take care of itself." Her hands slipped from the planes of his cheeks to his shoulders to give him a gentle shake. "*Please* say it, Beau."

"I'm *not* chivalrous, damn it," he said harshly. "If I was chivalrous do you think I'd have married you? I knew our marriage wouldn't have too much influence on the immigration red tape we'd have to go through. I didn't even do it to force you to accept my help as I told you. I was just so damn afraid of losing you I had to tie you to me any way I could. I was freeing you with one hand and binding you with ropes of steel with the other. I wanted an excuse to hang around and watch over you, be with you." His lips tightened. "I think you would have found that any potential male threat to my cause would have mysteriously disappeared. I wouldn't have been able to help myself." He laughed mirthlessly. "Some Galahad!"

"Well, I'm glad to see you're not completely noble," she said, her eyes twinkling. "I'll be

much more comfortable with the Beau I've come
to know in the last few days. Can't you fall just
a little further from the pedestal?" she coaxed
softly. "Come on, bribe me a little. Say you love
me."

"Kate, you're tearing me apart." His voice was
shaking. "I'm trying to do what's best for you."

"You're a very stubborn man." She sighed.
"*You're* what's best for me." She suddenly fell to
her knees in the sand, the silky white gown billowing gracefully about her. She reached for his
hand and tugged it imperiously. "Come down
here."

He obediently fell to his knees facing her, his
expression wary. "You're not thinking of seducing me again?"

"It's not a bad idea," she said with a cheeky
grin. "But I don't want you quibbling later about
undue influence. There'll be another time and
place for that." She took his other hand in hers.
"Now it's time for vows."

"Vows?" His expression became even more
wary.

"My vows." She smiled lovingly at him. "You
caught me off guard during the ceremony on

deck, but I'm ready now. I think they'll be as valid said here with just the two of us as if we had all those witnesses."

"Kate—"

"Shhh, it's my turn." Her hands tightened on his as she gazed directly into his eyes. "You say you've found honesty and generosity in me. I hope it's true, for I've found both of those qualities in you. I've also found humor and kindness, courage and understanding. You warm me like the sun, and when I'm with you I want to stretch out my arms and my heart and the spirit within that they call the soul." Her voice was soft but vibrantly alive. "For the rest of my life I'll give you what you want and need from me. I'll protect and guard, grow with you and beside you, hold your hand in comfort and your body in passion." She paused. "And I will love you until the day I die, Beau Lantry."

The soft breeze was lifting the curls at her temple and she was gazing at him with those clear loving eyes that didn't know how to lie. He could feel something deep inside him melt and ebb away and knew whatever it was, it would never return. He didn't know how they came together, but suddenly she was in his arms. "Oh, Lord, I *do* love you, Kate." His voice was a broken murmur and the cheek he pressed to hers was damp with tears. "I do! I do!"

"I know you do." Her tone was almost a maternal croon. "And it will be better now, you'll see." She kissed him gently, her hand stroking the hair back from his face. "I don't want you to be strong for me, just with me. If you want to give me all those things, I won't argue with you. I'll accept them gladly, but you've got to accept my gifts as well. For the rest of our lives we'll be giving each other all we have to give. It will be beautiful, Beau."

"Yes, beautiful." His voice was still husky but he didn't try to hide it. "You're very sure, Kate? You wouldn't want to try it my way for a few months?" His lips twisted. "I don't think there's any way I could let you have complete freedom now but I'd try to stay in the background as much as possible."

"And make us both miserable?" She shook her head. "No way. I intend to enjoy my honeymoon."

"I'll see that you do." His arms tightened and

he buried his lips in the curls at her temple. "I want to give you so much pleasure, Kate. I want to give you everything, be everything to you. I'd like to be your father and your brother, your friend and your lover." He tilted her chin to look into her eyes. "It seems that my entire life has been like that little carousel of yours, one long dizzy ride with the brass ring just out of reach. Now it's here, shining bright and true and it's *mine*."

The sun was almost down now and the rosy haze had turned to a mellow gold that touched everything with a clear radiance. Beau's eyes were golden now, too, and shining with the love he'd just admitted. It was too much. She buried her face in his shoulder once again. She tried to steady her voice into lightness. "So what now? Do we set sail on the *Searcher* and try to find Atlantis?"

His hand was gently stroking her hair. "I've been searching for Atlantis all my life, I think," he said quietly. "It's all a part of the carousel syndrome. No, I think we'll go to Briarcliff and visit Dany and Anthony. Then we'll go searching for something much more valuable."

"And what is that?"

"Purpose," he said slowly. "I'm beginning to think it may be the ultimate treasure." His lips brushed her temple. "After my Kate, of course."

"Of course," she said teasingly. "That does sound a terribly ponderous goal for a playboy with the instincts of a privateer. Daniel warned me that life around you might be a trifle boring from now on."

"I don't think you'll have to worry about any serious attacks of ennui. I'll guarantee to keep you interested." He chuckled with sudden mischievousness. "Besides, you shouldn't be so critical when my return to the straight and narrow is entirely your fault."

"My fault? I told you I didn't have the right to ask—"

"Your fault," Beau repeated. He kissed her lovingly on the lips. "How could the vagabond lifestyle of even the most determined pirate possibly survive when his lady is a combination of Xanthippe and the Queen of Sheba?"